CAUGHT

"I— It's— Oh my God," Gertie croaked.

Tess started back down the hall. Julian must have returned to the kitchen. She could think of nothing else that could have gotten Gertie so rattled. What in the world had the chef done now?

Gertie slumped against the door facing. "Help—me."

As Tess, Dahlia, and Cinny ran toward her, Tess saw something red on Gertie's right hand. Gertie lifted the hand and stared at it as if it were a foreign object she was amazed to see attached to her arm. Then Gertie made a gagging sound and swiped the hand down the front of her new pink dress, leaving a long stain.

Just as Tess reached her, Gertie moaned and slid slowly down until she sat, crumpled like a rag doll, against the door facing.

———

"She creates paperback masterpieces."
Tulsa World

Other Iris House B&B Mysteries by
Jean Hager
from Avon Books

BLOOMING MURDER
DEAD AND BURIED
DEATH ON THE DRUNKARD'S PATH
THE LAST NOEL
SEW DEADLY
WEIGH DEAD

JEAN HAGER

BRIDE
AND
DOOM

AN IRIS HOUSE
B&B MYSTERY

AVON BOOKS
An Imprint of HarperCollinsPublishers

AVON BOOKS
An Imprint of HarperCollins*Publishers*
10 East 53rd Street
New York, New York 10022-5299

Copyright © 2000 by Jean Hager
ISBN: 0-380-80376-3
www.avonbooks.com

First Avon Books paperback printing: November 2000

Avon Trademark Reg. U.S. Pat. Off. and in Other Countries, Marca Registrada, Hecho en U.S.A.
HarperCollins® is a trademark of HarperCollins Publishers Inc.

Printed in the U.S.A.

OPM 10 9 8 7 6 5 4 3 2 1

Chapter 1

Balancing several covered dishes on a tray, Tess Darcy backed up to the Victoria Springs Country Club's side entrance, using her body to push open the door. The entrance led down a hallway to the kitchen and the club's two dining rooms. Gertie Bogart, the Iris House cook, who was similarly laden, was right behind Tess.

"Gertie," Tess said over her shoulder, "this has been so much work for you. I can't thank you enough."

"I wouldn't have it any other way, Tess."

Gertie had insisted on preparing the buffet dinner for the forty guests who were expected in about an hour for Tess's bridal shower. Tess's Aunt Dahlia had received special permission from the club manager for Gertie to use the club's kitchen and china for the evening, thereby executing an end run around the temperamental club chef, Julian Walker, who didn't want anybody except his staff setting foot in "his" kitchen. In fact, Walker had been known, upon finding a member's guest in his domain, to order the stranger out.

"I can't believe there're only two weeks left till the wedding," Tess said, "and Dad and the family are coming in tonight. I barely had time to show the Stedmans to their room before we left Iris House."

1

"That's your father's old college friend and his wife?"

"Right. I heard Oliver Stedman tell his wife that Wayne Trammell had invited them out for dinner. Mrs. Stedman said she was too tired to go out. I guess Oliver will go alone." Wayne Trammell was another of her father's old college pals. The three—Trammell, Stedman, and Frank Darcy—had belonged to the same fraternity and had kept up with one another through the years since.

"Real nice of them to come for your wedding."

"That's not the main reason they're here, Gertie. Oliver Stedman owns some land the country club is interested in buying for the new golf course. Seeing Dad and Wayne Trammell is a big plus, but I think the wedding is incidental." She shifted the weight of her tray. "Anyway, I feel a little guilty about leaving Ruth Stedman at Iris House alone."

"If her husband was willing to, why should you feel guilty? Stop beating yourself up, Tess," Gertie advised.

Tess managed a weak smile. "You're right. I'll concentrate on the wedding, but if I let myself think about how much I still have to do, I get panicky."

"Now, Tess, just calm down. You know I'll help. Your Aunt Dahlia, Cinny, and your stepmother will lend a hand, too. Everything essential will get done."

"Thanks, Gertie. Keep telling me that." Gertie was right. She did have family to fall back on, unlike Luke, an only child whose parents were deceased. Gertie's down-to-earth practicality served as a steadying influence on Tess, an influence she needed as her wedding day approached.

Upon reaching the kitchen, Tess discovered to her dismay that the chef and his young assistant, Paula Overton, were still there and, it appeared, not planning to leave any time soon. A huge pot sat, warming, on the range, from which wafted the smell of barbecued meat. Paula stood at the island counter, chopping fresh cabbage. Additional signs of a large meal being prepared met Tess's gaze as it swept the room.

Walker glanced toward Tess, who had hesitated in the doorway. When he saw the tray of food she carried, his head shot up and he scowled fiercely. That scowl could make people who worked for him break out in a cold sweat. "What is *that*?" he demanded.

"Food for my bridal shower buffet," Tess explained and smiled gamely, hoping to make the best of an uncomfortable and unforeseen situation. "It's scheduled for seven o'clock in the main dining room." As he must surely know, since schedules of the week's events were posted in several places around the club, including the kitchen notice board. From where she stood, Tess could see the board next to the large refrigerator, the schedule prominently displayed in the center of the board.

For his own impenetrable reasons, the chef chose to pretend the shower was news to him. "Oh, really?"

Tess pointed at the notice board. "It's been on the schedule for several weeks." As you know, you arrogant jerk, she fumed silently.

Walker did not even look at the notice board. "I don't concern myself with events utilizing food from outside. Since the governing board frowns upon such activities, they are quite rare. I can't clutter my mind with trivialities."

If it's trivial, Tess thought, why are you so agitated? "Nevertheless," she said firmly, "we're on the schedule."

Walker dismissed her with a flick of his fingers. "You're scheduled in the dining room. Take your food in there. As you can see, we're busy here."

"I was told we'd have access to the kitchen—by the manager," Tess said. "In fact, I was under the impression we'd have the kitchen to ourselves."

"*This* kitchen?" he inquired with a snide curl of the thin upper lip barely visible beneath a luxurious, salt-and-pepper mustache. Tess had always suspected the mustache was there to disguise a miserly mouth too small for his long face.

"It's the only one in the building, isn't it?"

Rather than answer her obviously rhetorical question, he snapped, "Evidently, you were misinformed. This is the final day of the club golf tournament, and we're preparing a buffet that is also scheduled for seven, on the patio. It's the big event of the week." The last added, Tess was sure, to emphasize that her shower was somewhere down the list—Julian Walker's list, anyway.

Tess knew that Luke and her Uncle Maurice Forrest had played in the club tournament, but she hadn't known about the patio buffet. Since Wayne Trammell was an avid golfer, his dinner invitation for his old friend Oliver Stedman was probably for the barbecue. But the manager, Jed Baskin, had certainly known about the patio event, and he'd granted Tess the use of the kitchen. As for the chef, he would just have to make a little space for Gertie to prepare the shower meal.

When Tess did not turn away, Walker said, "You'll have to take your food elsewhere." Considering Tess summarily dismissed, he smoothed his mustache with thumb and index finger, then picked up two large containers of baked beans and slid them into one of the club's four ovens.

Tess was not going to be fobbed off by this petty dictator. "We need to put together a salad and heat some of the dishes." To give force to her words, she stepped to the end of the center work island where Paula was chopping vegetables and placed her tray on the counter. Paula gave her a wary look, perhaps meant as a warning. "We will also be using some of your china and flatware," Tess added. "We have permission from Jed Baskin for that as well. I'm sorry for the misunderstanding, but I'm sure we can work around you. Don't you think so, Gertie?"

She turned and found that Gertie had remained in the hallway and was half-hidden behind the open door. "Gertie?"

Gertie took a reluctant step into full view, looking as if she'd prefer to disappear. It was not Gertie's style to be a shrinking violet. What was wrong with her? Tess had never known Gertie to be subdued by anyone, much less another cook, even one with such a lofty opinion of himself. Gertie was widely considered the best cook in Victoria Springs, and Tess would put her up against Julian Walker any day of the week.

"You can bring that tray in here," Tess prompted.

Gertie placed her tray beside Tess's on the counter. In the better light of the kitchen and surrounded by white appliances and cabinets, Tess now saw that Gertie looked flushed, and she kept her eyes lowered. What on earth?

Walker had turned from the oven, stiff with indignation. Plainly he was not accustomed to having his word contradicted so blatantly in his domain.

His assistant, Paula, had moved to the sink, as far as she could get from the escalating confrontation and still remain in the kitchen. She was now peeling potatoes, her eyes averted.

Paula was serving a year's apprenticeship under Walker. From the few occasions when Tess had seen her at the club, the young woman seemed to be at pains to make herself unobtrusive. This was understandable, since Walker appeared to take any opportunity to berate her and critize her culinary abilities. Once Tess had even heard him say he must have taken complete leave of his senses when he agreed to oversee her apprenticeship. The man was a tyrant.

Walker took an aggressive step toward Tess, who stood her ground. "Don't you understand plain English, Miss Darcy? You cannot come in here!" His face was red with fury. This wasn't the first flare-up she'd witnessed from the chef. Walker had a short fuse. Apparently throwing a tantrum was a tactic that usually worked for him. Paula was clearly cowed by him and Gertie, uncharacteristically timid, seemed to be as well. Tess, however, had no intention of backing down. Glancing to one side, she mouthed, "Ignore him."

When she looked back at the chef, Walker's expression had undergone an amazing transformation. It was as if he were really seeing Gertie for the first time, and for an instant, he appeared to be struck dumb with his mouth hanging open. When he recovered, he pointed a long finger at Gertie, who lifted her head and glared at him. Her hazel eyes blazed. Tess had rarely seen her this angry—but why was she being so quiet about it? Maybe it was the country club setting that intimidated her.

"You!" Walker shouted.

"Don't yell at her," Tess said. "It's my shower. She's the cook at my bed and breakfast, and she's only here tonight as a favor to me. I don't understand your problem, Mr. Walker, but whatever it is, take it up with me."

Walker ignored her, turning to Paula. "Where in hell are those two boys you hired to help out this evening?"

Paula jumped at having his anger suddenly vented in her direction. "I'm sure they'll be here any minute."

"I knew I shouldn't have left hiring them up to you. Can't you do anything right, Paula? Frankly, I don't know how long I can put up with your bumbling."

Poor Paula went pale, but didn't respond. The chef returned his attention to Gertie and seemed surprised to find her still standing beside the work island. His eyes narrowed, and again, he raised a shaking finger to point at her. "Out!"

Of all the nerve! Tess gave up trying to keep her temper in check. "Now, see here. We have permission to use the kitchen and we're going to use it. Do I have to find the manager to settle this?"

"He's fully occupied, circulating among the guests on the patio. I'm sure he doesn't want to be bothered by your bridal shower."

"Too bad," Tess snapped. "I'm going to speak to him."

She added with an ironic little smile, "I'm sure he'll be glad to take time away from the guests to settle a kitchen dispute."

"No, *I* will take care of this," Walker snarled and stormed out of the kitchen.

Paula looked over her shoulder and lifted pale eyebrows at Tess. She was a petite woman, who would probably be attractive with makeup, her light brown hair released from the tight net she wore. "Mr. Baskin must've neglected to tell him you were coming."

"I don't believe that for a moment," Tess retorted. "He knew very well we'd be here."

Paula smiled apologetically. "Julian is very possessive about the kitchen."

"He'll have to get over it," Tess said shortly. "Come on, Gertie, let's take the dishes and silverware into the dining room."

Paula chuckled, as if the thought of Walker "getting over it" amused her. "There's a cart in the pantry," she said, indicating a closed door on one wall. "With that you can transport everything at once. I'm glad you stood up to him. Just don't tell him I said so."

Tess gave her a sympathetic look. "You have to stand up to bullies or they'll run right over you."

"Easy for you to say," Paula observed, "but you don't work for him."

"He has no right to treat you like slave labor. You should file a complaint with the manager."

She shook her head. "If I wash out of this apprenticeship, I'll have a very hard time getting another, a decent one, anyway. Despite his temperamental personality, Julian has a good reputation in places where it counts. He could blackball me."

Gertie snorted. "Good reputation! What a laugh. He ought to be run out of town on a rail."

Both Tess and Paula looked at her in surprise.

"What I mean is," she amended, "Tess, her fiance, and her aunt's family are members here. The chef is an employee. Somebody should remind him of that."

"I'm sure the manager will," Paula said. "Julian will come back in a worse temper than when he left."

"How long has he been here, anyway?" Gertie asked.

"About a year," Tess said. "Why?"

"Just wondering," Gertie said.

Paula sighed heavily. "I dread the rest of this evening."

"You don't have to put up with abuse," Tess said.

"I get through it by telling myself I only have to stay another eight months," Paula responded. "I have a calendar in my apartment where I mark off the days. I need a good recommendation from him at the end of the year if I'm to get employment as a chef." She frowned, and her face seemed to crumple. "Sometimes, like tonight, when he's in such a black mood, I'm sure he'll never let me stay long enough to finish the course."

"Would you like me to speak to Mr. Baskin for you?"

Paula looked alarmed. "Please don't."

"Whatever you want," Tess said, "but if you change your mind . . ."

"Thanks, but I can handle it."

Tess had not seen her handle the chef very well thus far, but it was none of her business. She went to the pantry and got the cart. With Gertie's help, she transferred forty place settings of china and silverware to it and wheeled it to the main dining room, which was situated across an open area from the kitchen. This was the room where brunch was served on Sundays, as well as other meals open to all members and guests. The long windows set into one wall looked out on the golf course. Another, less commodious dining room was situated on the other side of the kitchen and could be reached via the pantry as well as from the hallway. It was called the green room to distinguish it from the main dining area. Smaller functions were accommo-

dated there, such as the governing board's monthly luncheon and business meeting.

Somebody had already started preparations for the
shower. A buffet table against one wall was covered with
a white cloth. Matching napkins were stacked on one end
of the table, and in the center sat a beautiful arrangement
of daisies and salmon-colored roses. Small tables, each
accommodating four people, were scattered about the
room. These had been made ready with fresh white cloths
and bud vases, each containing a single salmon-colored
rose.

"Looks like Aunt Dahlia was here earlier," Tess
observed. Dahlia and Tess's cousin, Cinny, were
cohostessing the shower. "I hope she gets back before the
guests begin to arrive."

"Tess," Gertie said, "if I'd known about Julian Walker . . ."
She halted uncertainly and pursed her lips.

"Yes?" Tess prompted.

"I'm just not sure it's such a good idea to use the club
kitchen."

"There's nowhere else to heat the food and make a
salad."

"I could go back to Iris House and fix the salad, and
surely there's a microwave oven in this place besides the
one in the kitchen."

"Absolutely not," Tess said adamantly. "Julian doesn't
own that kitchen. As you said yourself, he only works here,
and Aunt Dahlia cleared it with the manager. I won't let
that man intimidate us."

Gertie studied her thoughtfully.

"What?"

Gertie hesitated, then said, "Nothing," and began
unloading the cart and arranging the china on the serving
table.

"Gertie, you haven't had previous dealings with Julian
Walker, have you?"

"What gave you that idea?" she muttered, carefully lining up forks.

"The way you acted in the kitchen."

"I was offended by his rude behavior toward you. The very idea, him treating you that way!"

Tess let it go, though she had a hunch there was more to Gertie's attitude than she was saying. She watched Gertie straighten up and run her hands down her ample form, smoothing her bright pink tent dress over her hips as she scanned the table arrangement.

"If you'd rather stay out of the kitchen . . ."

"No. I'll make the salad and take care of heating the dishes. I'll try to keep out of Julian Walker's way. You should be here to talk to your guests."

They heard high heels tapping in the hall, and Dahlia and Cinny Forrest breezed into the room. "Good evening!" Dahlia greeted them. She wore a soft lavender dress of summer silk with a single strand of pearls. As always, her frosted hair was perfectly coiffed. Cinny was attired in a butter-yellow linen suit with matching high-heeled pumps. Her long blond hair was pulled back in a coiled French braid. Both the Forrest women had bought new clothes for the occasion and looked elegant enough to be photographed for a fashion magazine cover.

Cinny gave Tess a hug. "I love that outfit," she said. "Blue is definitely your color." Tess also had a new dress, a sleeveless shantung fitted sheath with a matching waist-length jacket.

Cinny released Tess and turned to Gertie. "You look very nice, too, Gertie."

"Ummm—sorry, what did you say, Cinny?" Gertie asked, looking distracted.

"I was complimenting you on your dress. Is it new?" Like most of Gertie's dresses, this one was a loose A-line to accommodate her broad hips. She made them herself.

Gertie smiled fleetingly. "Yes, it is, and thank you, dear."

Dahlia walked over to survey the serving table. "I see you've brought in the dishes and flatware. How can I help, Gertie?"

"Not much left to do," Gertie said, "and I wouldn't want you to get a stain on your pretty dress. You relax. I'll take care of the meal."

Despite Gertie's caution, Dahlia went to the buffet table and began rearranging napkins and silverware.

"Aunt Dahlia," Tess said, "did you know the chef is serving a barbecue buffet on the patio this evening?"

Dahlia turned from her task to reply, "I didn't until today. Somehow the barbecue got left off the schedule for previous weeks. Somebody in the office goofed, I guess. Probably the new girl. Between the two of us, she always seems a bit scattered to me." A small frown etched itself between her arched brows. "Is Julian being difficult?"

"Yes," Tess said, "but I told him we had permission to use the kitchen from Jed Baskin. He wasn't impressed. He's gone to lodge a complaint with Jed."

"Can you believe it?" Cinny asked, shaking her head.

Dahlia rolled her blue-gray eyes. "Oh, that man! Well, he won't get anywhere with Jed, who knows which side his bread is buttered on. Maurice is on the governing board." She looked thoughtful. "I saw Wayne Trammell and the golf pro going into the green room as we passed." Trammell was chairman of the club's governing board. "I'll stick my head in and have a word with Wayne about the chef's attitude, if necessary."

"Let's wait and see what Jed tells Julian," Tess suggested.

"Yes, I hate to bother Wayne if it can be avoided. He's working with the firm designing the new golf course and has been negotiating for land. That's probably what he and the pro are discussing right now. There's been a lot of arguing back and forth among the board members over which site to make an offer for. The one Wayne favors is the best suited for the new course, according to the pro, but it's also the most expensive." She paused reflectively, then shook her head.

"That must be the acreage Oliver Stedman owns," Tess said.

"Ummm," Dahlia agreed. "Anyway, with that, and running his real estate business, Wayne's got plenty on his mind. Not to mention his demanding wife. Esther isn't the easiest woman in the world to live with."

"The last time Cody and I ate in the dining room, Wayne and Esther had the next table, and she spent the whole time complaining about the food, the service, everything," Cinny said.

"I can't imagine how Wayne has put up with her all these years," Dahlia added, "but you didn't hear me say that."

"I'm going to fix the salad," Gertie announced.

"I'll go with you," Dahlia told her, "just in case Julian is still on his high horse. Our chef needs to be taken down a notch or two every few weeks or he's impossible. This time, I suppose it's up to me to do it."

"Go get him, Mother," Cinny said with a laugh.

Dahlia nodded absently, then mused, "Julian isn't the most pleasant man on the planet at the best of times, but at the moment, there may be extenuating circumstances."

"Such as?" Tess asked.

"Oh, I just meant he may have personal reasons for being in a foul mood," Dahlia said mysteriously.

"What personal reasons?" Cinny asked.

Dahlia shook her head. "It's probably nothing, and at any rate, it's none of our business."

"Come on, Mother," Cinny urged, "Tell us."

"Yes, what have you heard?" Tess added.

"Never mind, you two. I don't like to spread gossip."

"Since when?" Cinny inquired with a quirk of her brows.

Dahlia gave her daughter a displeased look, then turned

to Gertie. "Come along, Gertie. We'll brave the lion's den together." Then she led the way out of the dining room.

Cinny glanced at Tess and observed, "She knows *something* juicy. I'm dying to know what it is."

"Well, she's obviously not going to tell us," Tess said.

"We'll get it out of her eventually," Cinny assured her.

Tess frowned slightly. "Extenuating circumstances. What circumstances could possibly justify Julian's behavior?"

Cinny shrugged. "You got me."

Chapter 2

Raylene Walker had had only one object in mind when she decided to come to the barbecue over Julian's objections. She knew that she had to make a decision very soon to resolve the situation in which she found herself. The fact that said situation had been brought about by her own reckless actions was beside the point now.

"It's not wise," Julian had said when he was trying to talk her out of coming tonight, "the wife of an employee mingling with the members. It simply isn't done, Raylene. It looks as if you're putting yourself above your station."

She could hardly believe her ears. If anybody held an inflated opinion of his station, it was her husband. At the beginning of their marriage, she had seen this as admirable self-confidence, a quality that she herself had lacked. Now she found his puffed-up pride tiresome, sometimes even embarrassing.

"My station, Julian?" she'd inquired. "And what is that?"

"You know very well what I mean."

What she knew—what she'd come to know since she'd married him four years ago in San Francisco—was that her fifty-four-year-old husband was not the suave, sophisticated man of the world she'd imagined as a twenty-three-year-old waitress struggling to make ends meet.

At seventeen, leaving the home of her alcoholic parents had seemed the most acceptable of the scanty options open to her. For the next six years, she'd managed to scrape by on a waitress's earnings, but at least her parents weren't stealing from her purse for alcohol, which they'd done regularly when she lived with them.

She had started work in a dump of a café, sometimes holding down two jobs—anything to escape the house she'd grown up in.

Landing in the coffee shop of a San Francisco hotel three years later had been a giant step up, at least as far as the environment and the customers were concerned. Wages plus tips came to more than she'd made at the café, too, but not enough more to improve her lifestyle in any significant way.

When the chef at the hotel showed an interest in her, she was flattered. And when he drove her in his BMW to his condo overlooking the bay, she was awed. Later, when she learned that the car was leased and that Julian spent every dime of his salary on his lifestyle, it hardly seemed to matter. His salary was a fortune to her at the time. When Julian proposed, saying he could provide for his wife and she would no longer have to wait tables, which would not look right for the chef's wife, by the way, Raylene didn't have to think twice about her answer.

A woman stopped in front of Raylene. "You're looking awfully pensive." Her voice startled Raylene out of her reverie.

She smiled, unable to remember the woman's name. "I'm a little tired."

Fortunately, the woman spotted a friend and moved away. Alone again, Raylene drifted back to her past.

By the time Julian proposed, she was weary beyond words. Weary of counting pennies to make ends meet, of living half the month on the leftovers she could carry home from the hotel kitchen at closing time.

Julian Walker had seemed a knight on a white horse who had rescued her from a life of poverty to which, before his arrival on the scene, she could see no end. It had been easy to convince herself she loved him. But she had confused gratitude with love because she hadn't known the difference. Now she did.

By the time they moved to Victoria Springs, Raylene, who was then twenty-seven, had realized that she and her husband had few interests in common and that a well-furnished, three-bedroom home could be a prison as well as an escape from hard work and money worries. Marriage had made Julian more frugal. They added monthly to a savings account, and Julian had taken out a life insurance policy. Her husband had turned fifty-four a couple of months ago. In six years, he'd be *sixty*. Now, whenever she looked at him, no white-knight image came to mind. Instead, she felt as if she couldn't get a deep breath, as if the walls of her house were closing in around her, and her first thought was: He's *old*.

So she'd gone against Julian's wishes. "I played in the tournament so I'm invited to the barbecue."

Her insistence on taking the club pro up on his offer of free golf lessons had been another bone of contention with Julian. Of course, he'd opposed her playing in the tournament, as well. Julian found fault with almost everything she wanted to do that involved other people with whom she might become friendly. "Wendy played, too," Raylene had pointed out. "She's the wife of an employee and she's going."

"I know you and Wendy played in the tournament," Julian said, "but Wendy's husband is the golf pro. Johnny was in charge of the tournament." He spoke with deliberate slowness, as if he were explaining something obvious to a slow-witted child.

"So? You're the chef who's preparing the barbecue. I don't see the difference."

At that, Julian had left the house, his parting shot being

that it was impossible to reason with her lately, punctuated by a slammed door to let her know how angry he was. He must have expected that to change her mind about the barbecue. Which was why, when he came out on the patio and saw her there, he looked startled and then angry again. It didn't bother Raylene all that much, as Julian was often in a bad temper these days. More than often, really; he'd become a perpetually dour, sour man.

She merely waved at him from her chair, and he turned his back and wound his way through the clumps of golfers around the portable bar. He was clearly looking for someone, didn't find him or her, and went back inside without another glance at his wife.

There would be hell to pay tonight at home, but Raylene had more urgent concerns to deal with first. However, it was beginning to look as if it would be impossible to have a private word with anybody at the barbecue. Besides, the person she'd come to see had not yet put in an appearance.

She swallowed a sip of club soda to ease the tight dryness in her throat and wondered how she'd let herself get into such a dilemma. She hadn't meant to hurt anyone, really. She'd only wanted a new interest to relieve her restlessness, a temporary solution requiring a few little white lies, no real harm done, as long as she was careful.

But Raylene knew the real lie was the one she'd been telling herself. And the evidence of this was in the phone call she'd received a week ago and the stone that had been lodged in her stomach ever since.

Wendy Linzy, who was seated beside Raylene, suddenly turned from a conversation she was having with a man on her other side and placed a cool hand on Raylene's bare arm. It startled Raylene and made her shiver. She'd been so absorbed in her thoughts that she'd forgotten about Wendy, a mistake she'd been making a lot lately.

"You're awfully quiet this evening," Wendy said.

"Tired, I guess." Raylene studied Wendy's long face, wondering, not for the first time, what kind of marriage she and Johnny had. The sporty, outdoorsy type, Wendy golfed, fished, and jogged. She'd spent so much time in the sun, in fact, that at forty her complexion had a leathery overtanned look, and permanent lines fanned out from her brown eyes and scored her forehead and the corners of her mouth. She looked older than forty, whereas her husband, who was thirty-three, looked younger than his age.

To give her credit, Wendy was one of the few people in town who'd befriended Raylene, inviting her over for coffee several times, always when the Linzys' four-year-old son was at preschool.

Raylene knew that Wendy and Johnny had been married for five years, and that Wendy, an only child, came from money. Raylene suspected that the Linzys' expensive house on the golf course had been paid for by Wendy's father.

Johnny's salary was in the same ballpark as Julian's. The Walkers, who were childless, lived in a residential area three miles from the club because they couldn't afford to live on the course, where the lots alone were priced from seventy to a hundred thousand, and the Linzys' house sprawled over one of the largest plots in the development.

The value of all the land around the country club had skyrocketed in the last few years. The governing board was in the process of trying to buy land for another golf course, and Raylene had heard Wayne Trammell, chairman of the board, lamenting the fact that they hadn't had enough foresight to buy up more land years ago.

Frowning, Wendy gazed toward the patio doors. "Johnny and Wayne must have their heads together again about the new golf course. I may have to go after Johnny if he doesn't show up soon."

Wendy's husband, the golf pro, had worked with the architect to design the new course and was on the site selection committee. Wendy had told Raylene that the asking price on the site the board favored was more than two million dollars. Wendy tossed off such numbers as if she were talking about her grocery budget. Raylene couldn't even imagine how much money two million dollars was.

Just then, the assistant chef, Paula Overton, and two teenage boys hired for the evening to help in the kitchen came out on the patio with the buffet food on a cart. She recognized one of the boys as a wrestler on the local high school team. Good-looking kid. Craig, she thought his name was. Raylene had become casual friends with his mother, who had also been taking golf lessons from Johnny Linzy, and had accompanied her to one of the boy's matches. It was on a night when Julian had been tied up at the club, and she'd thought anything would be better than sitting home, watching television. Young, healthy males in next-to-nothing had been a pleasant change from her husband's wrinkled skin and belly paunch. But wrestling, it turned out, wasn't Raylene's cup of tea, and she'd declined the woman's second invitation.

As Craig and the other boy lifted big pans to the buffet table, the display of their youthful biceps was a sight she would have enjoyed had the smell of the barbecued meat not created a queasy tremor in her stomach.

"I saw your tournament scores," Wendy said now. "Your game is improving."

"It had nowhere to go but up—or down, I should say," Raylene replied. From the corner of her eye, she noticed two men—Johnny Linzy and Wayne Trammell—walking around the corner of the building toward the patio. They halted to greet a man who came toward them over the lawn. Raylene didn't recognize the third man.

"There's my wandering husband," Wendy said, jumping to her feet. People were already lining up for the buffet. "You coming, Raylene?"

"I think I'll wait till that line gets shorter. I'm not very hungry, anyway."

"Well, I'm famished," Wendy said. She gestured toward the folding chairs scattered about the lawn. "Shall I save you a chair with Johnny and me?"

"Never mind," Raylene said. "I'll find a spot somewhere when I'm ready."

"Whatever," Wendy said offhandedly. She circled around the buffet table to Johnny's side and linked her arm through his, leaning close to say something that made Johnny smile.

Raylene lowered her gaze and let it fall to her hands, which were clasped tightly in her lap. The knuckles were white, and she made a mental effort to relax her fingers.

She turned to look out at the golf course, now shrouded by evening shadows. With dusk, the day's heat had dissipated a little, and she took a deep breath, drawing in cooling air to ease her queasiness. The country club was set among manicured golf greens, gently rolling hills, and stately old trees. A beautiful spot, and though she liked to pretend otherwise, she knew she didn't belong there—with these people, most of whom were life-long residents of the town and civic leaders, and all of whom were, if not wealthy, at least comfortably well-off. They were relaxed with each other. They'd probably grown up taking it for granted that, like their parents, they'd be a part of the country club clique when they established their own homes. They reminded Raylene of some of the self-assured kids she'd gone to high school with, kids who had ignored her, passing her in the hall without a glance, as if she didn't exist.

Suddenly Raylene wanted to get up, go to her car, and drive away, past the lush country club lawns, the expensive houses, and right on out of town. But where would she go? She would have to stop sometime, and running away would not resolve her problem; it would only delay the inevitable.

She took a deep, shuddering breath. She dreaded what she had to do, but maybe it wouldn't be as bad as she expected. She gathered up her resolve. Had she really been living in a fantasy the past few months? Surely she couldn't have been totally blind to reality. She wouldn't let herself believe that. So maybe a fantasy ending was not too much to hope for. She slammed an imaginary door shut on that thought, remembering what her grandmother used to say—be careful what you hope for. Now was not the time to get cold feet.

She glanced toward the buffet line and caught him looking at her, tried to read his expression, but couldn't because he turned away so quickly. Nevertheless, her decision was made; she felt resigned. The stone in her stomach grew heavier.

He had hoped she wouldn't come tonight. He could handle it if she weren't staring at him every time he looked her way. How could other people not notice?

She'd taken to phoning him at work, too, even though he'd told her never to do that. Don't call me, I'll call you, he'd said at least a dozen times. But she claimed that sometimes she just needed to hear his voice. Women. They all wanted to possess you in the end, and on their terms.

The whole thing had gotten out of hand. It was time to put a stop to it. The problem was, he didn't know what she might do. He'd have to be very careful how he broke it to her.

Someone nudged him from behind. He was holding up the line. He removed his hands from his pockets and picked up a plate. Dipping into the baked beans, he could feel her eyes on his back.

It was just sex, he reminded himself, and now it was over. It wasn't his fault she'd built some female dream on a few rolls in the sack made more exciting because they were clandestine. Women always had to make it more than it was, or they'd feel used. It could never be just sex with them. Had it never occurred to her that she was using him, too?

Chapter 3

Returning to the dining room, Dahlia said, "The chef just now thundered into the kitchen looking like a tornado about to wreak havoc. He lit into a teenage boy who was hired for the evening—just because he was there, I guess. Julian said the boy was late and not to expect further employment at the club. The poor kid looked as if he didn't know what had hit him."

"Jed must have told Julian to leave Gertie alone," Cinny said, grinning. "As we all knew he would. I can't imagine Julian expected anything else."

"He's arrogant enough to think Jed would take his side," Tess observed.

"True," Cinny agreed. "I would love to have overheard that conversation."

"Are you sure it's wise to leave Gertie alone in the kitchen with him?" Tess asked.

"Don't worry, Tess," Dahlia advised. "Gertie's tough. She'll go about her business and ignore him."

Tess frowned. "The chef is fairly hard to ignore. And Gertie acted half-afraid of him when we arrived. Of course, he was incredibly rude. He actually ordered her out of the kitchen."

"Unbelievable," Dahlia observed. "Well, I tried to smooth his feathers. Told him how much Maurice and

I appreciate his letting us use the kitchen, as if he had any real say in the matter. Anything to get through the evening."

Tess said warmly, "That should help." If anyone could still troubled waters, it was Dahlia. She'd had plenty of practice, serving on various civic committees.

"I've been meaning to ask, Tess," Dahlia said. "Would you like me to drive to Springfield after the shower and pick up Frank and Zelda and the kids?"

"Sweet of you to offer," Tess said, "but Dad's getting a rental car at the airport. They'll need transportation while they're here, and I can't turn my car over to them. Too much last-minute running around to do."

Cinny had been wandering about the room, checking things out. "Where are we going to put the gifts?"

"Oh, dear." Dahlia sighed. "Jed was supposed to have one of those round tables in the small dining room brought in." She shook her head. "Come on, Cinny. We'll have to get it ourselves."

"While you do that," Tess said, "I'll go see how Gertie is getting along."

Nobody was in the kitchen when Tess got there. Paula and the boys hired to help were probably on the patio, but where were Julian and Gertie? She hesitated in the middle of the kitchen for a few moments, trying to decide where they might have gone. As she was about to leave, she heard voices coming from behind the closed pantry door.

"You were spying on me!" the chef said, his voice low, but tense with repressed outrage.

"Don't be ridiculous," Gertie retorted stoutly. Tess was not surprised that Julian was still causing trouble, even after conferring with the club manager. And apparently Dahlia's attempt to calm him down hadn't worked, either. But she was relieved to know that Gertie had decided to stand up to him.

"I knew I shouldn't have let you stay here!"

"I don't think you had anything to do with that decision. I'll bet the manager put you in your place."

"You don't know what you're talking about! Not that *that* surprises me."

"Look, I don't want to argue with you. I've got work to do, so leave me alone."

"Not so fast. How much of my conversation did you hear?" the chef demanded.

"When?"

"A few minutes ago, when you were eavesdropping."

"I wasn't eavesdropping!" Gertie insisted. "I just walked in here. I heard muffled voices, but I couldn't understand what was being said. Furthermore, I'm not the least bit interested in anything *you* have to say."

"You haven't been given leave to wander through the club at will," Walker told her. "You have no business being in the pantry."

"I'm looking for a knife to cut the cake with," Gertie said. "I guess this butcher knife will have to do."

"Put that down. Here's a cake knife. Take it and get out of my pantry!"

"*Your* pantry? You seem to have a bad habit of claiming what belongs to other people as your own."

"How dare you!" Walker's tone rose and turned menacing. "I should have sued you two years ago!"

"Why didn't you?"

"I felt sorry for you."

"Sure you did," Gertie snorted. "The truth is you didn't sue me because you didn't want to be investigated yourself."

"That was my mistake, but it's not too late to sue. If I get the slightest inkling that you're spreading your vicious lies here, I'll take you to court. A chef's reputation is his most valuable asset."

"A reputation based on cheating will fail eventually." With that, Gertie pushed open the swinging pantry door and stalked into the kitchen, a cake knife clutched in her fist. Her face flushed, she came to an abrupt halt when she saw Tess.

"Gertie?"

Gertie gave a quick shake of her head and walked past Tess and out of the kitchen.

Julian Walker rushed out of the pantry, came to a dead stop, and glared at Tess. "I can't believe you'd have a woman like that working for you, Miss Darcy."

"I'm lucky to have her. Gertie would have no trouble at all getting another job, should she ever want to leave Iris House which I hope never happens. She's a wonderful cook and my friend."

Walker merely sniffed disdainfully and turned his back on Tess to get something from the refrigerator.

"What did you mean when you said you should have sued Gertie two years ago?"

"Your cook is such a good *friend*. Ask her," Walker retorted, still not looking at Tess.

"I'm asking you, Julian."

He closed the refrigerator door with a thud and whipped around to face her. "I may have to tolerate that woman in my kitchen for the evening, Miss Darcy, but I don't have to give you my life story. Now, if you'll excuse me, I need to see how things are progressing on the patio."

He left as Cinny came into the kitchen by another door. "What happened in here?' Cinny asked. "Gertie is mumbling that Julian Walker is a big fraud, but she won't explain what she means." She glanced toward the door by which the chef had exited. "I think Walker's opinion of Gertie is about the same. What gives, Tess?"

"I wish I knew. When I came in here, Gertie and Walker were in the pantry with the door closed. They were having an extremely heated conversation. Gertie called him a cheater and Julian threatened to sue her."

"For calling him names?" Cinny laughed. "He's just blowing off steam. He'd never get a lawyer to take on a suit like that. And if he did, the judge would throw it out of court and probably lecture Julian about clogging up the system with frivolous charges."

"I think there's more to it than that," Tess said thoughtfully. "Julian referred to something that happened two years ago."

"That was before he came to Victoria Springs. Gertie couldn't have known him then."

"I asked her earlier if she'd known him before. Now that I think back on it, she was evasive. She didn't really answer my question." Tess scowled in perplexity. "Gertie has lived here most of her life, hasn't she?"

Cinny nodded. "I went through school with her youngest son."

"Two years ago," Tess mused. "That was about the time I moved to Victoria Springs. Where was Gertie working before I hired her?"

"She was doing catering out of her home. She'd been doing that for at least ten years. Had as much business as she could handle, too. I know Mother used her several times, and she always had to make sure she got on Gertie's schedule early. For last-minute affairs, she had to find somebody else. You were fortunate to get Gertie at Iris House."

"I know it. But if she was catering here in town two years ago, I don't see how she could have run into Walker. He came to Victoria Springs from San Francisco."

"The plot thickens."

"Indeed it does." Tess laughed softly. "I hate it when people keep secrets."

"You're like me. Mother says I'm too nosy for my own good."

"I'm sure she'd say the same about me," Tess said. "Must be our Darcy blood."

"Which Mother shares."

Tess acknowledged this with an arched brow.

Cinny went on, "Mother hinted that she knows secrets about Julian and now Gertie's doing it. Everybody is being mysterious tonight." Cinny lifted linen-clad shoulders. "You don't suppose they're doing it just to drive us crazy, do you?"

Tess made a helpless gesture with her hands.

"Frankly," Cinny went on, "I don't understand any of it."

"Nor do I. I'll try to get Gertie to tell me more later."

"And I'll work on Mother. Now, we better get back to the shower. Several women arrived as I was leaving the dining room."

"Already?" Tess glanced at her watch. Where had the last hour gone?

"I'm just sorry Zelda and Maddie didn't get to town in time to come tonight," Cinny said.

"Me, too, but Dad said it was the earliest flight they could get today. I'll tell them all about the shower and they can inspect the gifts later," Tess said abstractedly, still trying to make sense of the overheard exchange between Gertie and Julian Walker.

Cinny took her arm as they left the kitchen. "Come along, cuz. It's show time."

Several women descended on Tess as soon as she arrived in the dining room, offering congratulations and hugs. For the time being, she put aside her questions about Gertie and the chef to enjoy her bridal shower.

Johnny Linzy's life had taken a downhill turn the moment he'd agreed to be on the site selection committee. At the time, he'd been flattered, and, after all, it made sense for the club pro to be in on decisions affecting the new course. All very simple and reasonable, he'd thought.

Still, it had made him feel as though he'd gone up a notch or two in the eyes of the board. He'd even bragged about it to his father-in-law, who seemed to be around more and more of late, saying the governing board had expressed great confidence in his opinions.

The old man had greeted this announcement by helping himself to Johnny's scotch and proclaiming, "Have you ever thought of going on the PGA tour, John? A chance of making decent money there. Have to take risks if you're ever going up in this world."

It was the old man's way of telling him he wasn't impressed by the board's confidence in Johnny, who was, after all, little more than a servant to the club members. Wendy's widowed father had not approved of Johnny as a husband for his daughter, and he rarely lost an opportunity to let Johnny know he hadn't changed his mind about that.

Johnny was getting damned tired of the old man's driving down from the Chicago suburb where Wendy grew up and showing up at the Linzy house without notice. You'd think he owned the place, and maybe he felt that he did since he'd bought the lot the house sat on and contributed another fifty thousand for the rambling house Wendy had insisted they build. Even then, the monthly mortgage payments were a heavy drain on the Linzys' budget.

Johnny would have been satisfied with a modest home, one more in keeping with his income. It was true, when he married Wendy, he'd known she would eventually inherit a lot of money. Maybe that had even been a factor in his decision to propose, though he didn't like to think that of himself. But he'd been willing to wait, and he'd thought Wendy was, too. But after Marcus was born, she began finding fault with their lifestyle.

"There's nothing wrong with the way we live, darling," he'd told her. "We have all we need for now."

To which she'd replied derisively, "I'm sick of counting pennies. We can't even afford a house cleaner once a week. And I *hate* this house. It's too small, now that there are three of us."

"I hadn't thought about it—"

"Of course not. You're not shut in here with the baby all day."

"Is it really that awful for you?" Her stony stare was answer enough. "I guess we could look for another house.

There's a brick ranch in the next block that just went up for sale. From the outside, it looks a little bigger than ours."

"I don't want a house in the next block. I want to build one on the golf course."

"You know we can't afford that."

"Daddy will help us," she'd said.

Of course, she'd already talked to her father about it. He knew that from the way she announced that she wanted a house on the course, as if the words had been waiting at the back of her mouth for the right moment to spew out.

Wendy and her father had already made the decision, so there was no point in trying to change her mind. And Johnny really couldn't blame his wife for her attitude. She'd been given the best of everything, growing up—more toys than any child could play with, private schools, a new convertible when she turned sixteen, and later, a Yale education. She'd played at working for a few years following her graduation from the university, but after her mother's death, she'd quit her job, moved in with her father, and taken over management of the house and servants.

She wasn't used to being denied. What Johnny couldn't give her, her father was perfectly willing to provide, and she saw no reason not to take advantage of that.

He had come to despise Wendy's father and had been determined to get himself and his family out from under the old man's thumb. Which was why he'd been so easily led down the treacherous path where he now found himself. The architect the board had chosen to design the course, an opinionated SOB, had not helped his cause, either.

But ultimately it was his wife's fault, he told himself, his wife who insisted on breezing in and out of the country club as if she were a member in good standing, instead of the wife of an employee.

Well, he could do nothing about that, either. If he brought up the subject, she'd just get her father to buy a membership, changing her status to the daughter of a member.

It was in this frame of mind that Johnny slipped around the building to enter the club, unnoticed, by a side door. His wife was engaged in conversation with several of the golfers. He could be back on the patio before Wendy missed him.

Chapter 4

Two and a half hours later, the last of the shower guests were departing and Luke had come in from the barbecue, which was breaking up as well, to help Tess pack their gifts. Dressed in shorts and a knit shirt, a blond forelock falling across his forehead, he looked relaxed and healthily tanned, and very handsome.

"What a haul," he observed as he surveyed the gifts displayed on a table.

"Isn't it wonderful?" Tess asked, planting a kiss on his cheek. He smelled of the musky aftershave that she loved. "We got eight place settings of our silver and crystal," she told him, "and more small appliances than we can use since I already have some of them. We can trade them in for china."

He pulled her to him and kissed her properly, then held her away from him to look at her. "You're beautiful."

"Thank you, sweetheart." Tess brushed a tangle of auburn curls away from her face. "I am so glad that love is blind."

"I thought you were beautiful the first time I ever saw you—before I fell in love with you, which didn't happen until at least the second or third time. Now, shall I put the loot in your car?"

31

Tess shook her head. "I need to stay and help Aunt Dahlia and Cinny. Would you mind putting the gifts in your car and unloading them at Iris House?"

"No problem."

"Just stack them in the living room. Oh, and there's a woman, Ruth Stedman, in the Anabel Jane Room."

"Yeah, I met her husband at the barbecue."

"Be careful not to frighten Ruth. Her husband may not have returned to Iris House yet."

"I'll use the side door to our quarters. She'll never know I was there." He flashed a smile. "*Our* quarters. I love the sound of it."

The builders had finished the remodeling of Tess's apartment on the ground floor of Iris House last week, knocking out walls and doubling the floor space. She and Luke now had four bedrooms, two and a half baths, commodious living room, dining room, and kitchen. Her office was where it had always been, and her former sitting room had been turned into a den.

Tess's worries that the new addition would look "stuck on" to the old Victorian house had turned out to be groundless. The architect had done a marvelous job incorporating new with old.

From the outside, you would never guess that the house wasn't exactly as it had been constructed by the original builders.

With Cinny's help, they made several trips out to Luke's Jaguar, packing boxes into every available space, leaving only the driver's seat vacant. "I'd better go help Mother and Gertie," Cinny said.

As Cinny left, Luke began resettling the boxes piled in the passenger seat. Tess said, "I'll bring out the last few things, Luke."

She ran back inside and hurried along the hallway. Low voices in what seemed to be a tense exchange came from the green room, but the door to the hallway was closed and Tess couldn't see who was inside.

Gertie, Dahlia, and Cinny were clearing dishes and carting them back to the kitchen.

Tess grabbed the last of the gifts. "I'll be right back to help," she told her aunt.

"Tess," Dahlia said, "you look exhausted. You should go home with Luke."

"I wouldn't dream of abandoning you with all this work to do."

"We'll have things put to rights in no time. If you won't go home, then sit down and rest while we take care of this. It's bad luck for the bride-to-be to clean up after her own shower."

Tess gazed at her, amused. She was sure Dahlia had made that up. "I am tired," she admitted. "But wasn't it a terrific shower? Thank you so much, Aunt Dahlia. You, too, Cinny. I'll—" She halted, realizing that she'd been about to reveal Cinny's secret.

"What?" Cinny asked.

"Never mind. I'm so tired I don't know what I'm saying."

Dahlia pulled a chair away from one of the tables. "We were more than happy to host your shower, dear. Now, take those boxes out and then sit down here. You can supervise."

Tess went back outside and said good-bye to Luke. He climbed into his car and stuck his head out to ask, "When do you expect your family?"

"Not for a few hours yet. I hope I can keep my eyes open until they arrive."

He started the engine. "Later, love."

Tess returned to the dining room, where Cinny and Dahlia were loading more dishes on a tray. Tess started to help, but Dahlia swatted her hand lightly. "Sit down," she ordered.

Offering no further resistance, Tess sank into the chair

Dahlia had placed to one side of the door. Propping both elbows on her knees, she rested her chin in her hands and closed her eyes, thinking that, when she'd thanked Dahlia and Cinny for the shower, she'd almost said she wanted to plan Cinny's bridal shower as soon as her cousin announced her engagement to Cody Yount, a young attorney. Nobody knew about the couple's plans except Tess and Luke, and they'd been sworn to secrecy.

Cinny was not yet wearing her engagement ring. She and Cody had decided to wait until after Tess and Luke's wedding to make an official announcement. As Cinny had said to Tess, her mother, who loved planning social functions, would go into orbit with two weddings to think about. Thank goodness, Tess had caught herself before she let the cat out of the bag.

She sighed wearily as she remembered that tomorrow she had to meet with Julian Walker to work out the last details for the wedding buffet. After his inexcusable behavior this evening, she wished she'd hired a caterer from outside. But she'd known the chef would be displeased with Gertie's providing the shower meal and she hadn't wanted to deliver a second slight so soon after the first.

Being displeased with Gertie's presence and being downright mean about it were two different things, however, but it was too late to find another caterer now. She'd simply have to deal with Julian.

She heard Cinny and Dahlia leaving for the kitchen, but didn't open her eyes until, moments later, quick footsteps sounded in the hall outside the dining room. Raylene Walker, the chef's young wife, walked past the open doorway, her head down. Seconds later, she walked back the way she'd come.

This time Tess caught a glimpse of her face. Raylene looked unhappy, and Tess wondered if her husband had vented some of his anger in Raylene's direction. Why had such an attractive young woman married a man twice her age and with a violent temper to boot? Did the gossip

Dahlia had referred to earlier have anything to do with Raylene?

Oh, well, Tess had enough to think about these next two weeks without taking on the Walkers' problems, if indeed they had any. For all she knew, Julian was a real pussycat at home. Finding that impossible even to imagine, Tess smiled to herself.

As her eyes drifted shut again, she heard voices—a man's and a woman's. They seemed to be coming from the end of the hallway outside the dining room, the direction Raylene had just gone.

"I told you I couldn't talk to you here," the man said. "For God's sake, don't you know the meaning of the word 'discretion'?"

Tess didn't recognize the voice.

"I can't worry about discretion," the woman said, her voice trembling. It was Raylene Walker. She went on to say something else, her tone urgent but so low that Tess couldn't decipher the words.

"Don't try to pull that on me. I'm not seventeen years old, so your lies won't work!" the man said.

"I'm not lying."

There was a moment's silence, then the man said, "If it's true, then you brought it on yourself. It wouldn't surprise me if this isn't one of your calculated maneuvers. I want nothing to do with it."

"Oh, that is so typically male!" Raylene's quivering voice rose. "And this is *not* a maneuver, as you call it. I'm as stunned as you are, but I have nowhere else to turn."

"Keep your voice down," the man cautioned.

"I thought I knew you! I—I can't believe you're being so cruel. Have the past few months really meant nothing to you?"

"We had a little fun, Raylene. Don't try to turn it into the big romance of the century. The fact is, it should never have happened. I wish it hadn't, but it did—and now it's time to move on."

"Move on? Move *on*!"

"It's finished, Raylene," he hissed, "and for God's sake, keep your voice down."

"You never treated me this way before. Your feelings can't have changed overnight."

"You don't know anything about my feelings."

"You can't tell me you never had any feelings for me because I will never believe that."

"Believe what you want, but the only feeling I have right now is that your recklessness has become a big problem."

"Believe me, I never wanted it to come to this. But now that it has, we have to deal with it together."

"Read my lips, Raylene. There is no *us*. This has nothing to do with me. Don't try to bring me into it. Just handle it yourself—and be discreet about it. Don't call me again. Don't come here looking for me. I won't change my mind."

"Please—"

"No. I'm leaving now. Don't follow me."

The sound of Raylene's wracking sobs reached Tess, and she went to the door to peer down the hallway. The door at the end of the hall was closing behind the man, whoever he was, and Raylene Walker stood in the dim light, sobbing, her hands over her face.

Tess walked toward her. "Raylene, can I help?"

Raylene's head shot up at the sound of Tess's voice. Her eyes darted to Tess. "Where did you come from?"

Tess indicated the open dining room door. "My bridal shower's just finished." She took in Raylene's tearstained face and devastated eyes with concern. "Is there anything I can—?"

"No," Raylene cut her off.

"I'm sorry—I—"

"Leave me alone!" Raylene circled around Tess and for the second time, hurried down the hallway in the opposite direction.

Watching Raylene's retreating figure, Tess slowly

returned to the dining room. She sank into the chair, trying to think where she'd heard the man's voice before. For one instant at the end, it had seemed faintly familiar, but the identity of the speaker continued to elude her. He'd been speaking in low tones, hardly above a hoarse whisper, so it could easily have been a voice she would know under normal circumstances.

Cinny came back in and began pulling tablecloths off tables. "Mother and Gertie are winding up in the kitchen," she said. "I'll take these down to the laundry room and we can all go home."

Tess got up to help. "I'll go with you."

Cinny didn't argue. The laundry room was in a dark corner of the basement, and, no doubt, she was glad for Tess's company. As they walked toward the basement stairs, their arms full of table linens, Cinny said, "Julian's wife came in the kitchen and said she needed to speak to him privately. I think she'd been crying. He told her he'd talk to her later and she left."

If Julian had been in the kitchen, then it wasn't his voice Tess had heard at the end of the hallway. Besides, Julian had a unique way of raising his tone at the end of sentences, and the man she'd heard hadn't done that.

For a moment, Tess pondered the various small, tragic dramas that must have been going on at the club while she and her guests celebrated the happy occasion of Tess's approaching marriage.

"I saw Raylene in the hall," Tess said. "She talked to someone whose voice I didn't recognize, then began crying."

"Probably lamenting the fact that she married that man," Cinny observed. "I know I would be if I were in her shoes."

"Hmm, I've often wondered why she chose a husband so much older than she."

"It's not the age difference I wonder about," Cinny said, "but I'll bet he treated her differently before the wedding."

"Undoubtedly," Tess agreed.

Cinny shook her head. "As I left the kitchen, Julian went in search of his wife. I hope Mother and Gertie can finish in there before he comes back. All he's been doing is standing around, scowling at everybody and biting Paula's head off. He actually threatened to fire her."

"She must be used to that by now," Tess said as they started down the basement stairs.

"I suppose," Cinny murmured, adding after a moment, "It's always so dark down here. Where's the switch? Oh, here it is."

Light exposed the gray concrete floor and white appliances of the laundry room.

Cinny glanced at Tess. "Let's get rid of these linens and get out of here."

Chapter 5

On the patio, Wendy Linzy approached her husband. "I've been looking all over for you."

The crowd on the patio was thinning out. Johnny lifted a hand to wave at a couple who were leaving, and called, "I'll order that new putter tomorrow, George." To his wife, he said distractedly, "I had to talk to a couple of board members. They're going to decide on the golf course site at their next meeting. They want me to be there to make the case for the land to the south."

"Does it really matter so much if they don't choose the site you want?"

"I've explained this to you, Wendy," he said impatiently. "It's by far the best site."

"But the most expensive."

Strange to hear those words coming out of his wife's mouth. Usually, she wanted the most expensive of everything, but then the site of the new course would have no effect on her, none that she was aware of, at any rate. "Not that much more expensive."

"Well, you have the chairman and several other members on your side. I'm sure it will all work out for the best in the end."

"Why do you always think things will work out for

the best?" he snapped. But he knew why. Things had always worked out for Wendy. She led a charmed life.

She patted his arm. "Why do you always expect the worst?"

He pulled his arm away from her touch. "The site selection has become a political issue with the club members. I've pressed so hard for my choice that if the board decides against it, I could look foolish. My job could be in jeopardy."

Before she could reply, a woman interrupted to ask when Johnny could work in a couple of lessons for her. "I'm hooking half my shots lately," she explained. "I want you to help me correct my swing."

"Let me call you tomorrow, Mrs. Daly," Johnny said, his tone laced with patience, so different from the tone he'd been using with Wendy just now. "I have to look at my schedule in the office."

"Good," the woman said and wandered off in search of her husband.

"Johnny," Wendy said then, "you know you needn't worry about your job."

"I can't discuss this now," he snapped. "Excuse me. I have to talk to somebody before we go."

With a bewildered frown, Wendy watched him leave the patio and enter the building, his pace hurried. He'd been going back and forth all evening, too restless to be still for more than a few moments at a time. In fact, Johnny hadn't been himself for a while now. Lately he had seemed absorbed in a world of his own, even when he was with her and their son. Half the time, he didn't hear her when she spoke to him. And once he did, he reacted impatiently, as if she were an unwanted interruption. He'd even lashed out at Marcus, their four-year-old son, a few times, which wasn't like him. He adored Marcus.

Perhaps she should ask her father to have a word with him.

* * *

In the basement, Tess and Cinny dumped the linens in a basket and retraced their steps. As they started up the stairs, they heard an angry voice. There was no doubt in Tess's mind this time to whom it belonged—Julian Walker. It sounded as if he was standing in the hall at the top of the stairs, where Raylene and another man had been earlier.

Tess grabbed Cinny's arm. "Wait," she whispered. "They'll be embarrassed if they know we've heard them."

Cinny smiled. "We wouldn't want them to be embarrassed, now, would we?" she whispered back.

Then Tess recognized Raylene's voice mumbling something indistinct.

At the top of the stairs, Julian spat out, "You are such a liar!"

Cinny looked at Tess with wide eyes, and Tess gave a sad shake of her head. Clearly Julian was as mean to his wife as he was to everybody else.

"Julian, you may not want to believe me," Raylene wheedled. "But I'm not lying. I've known it for a week. I've just been waiting for the right time to tell you."

"And you think tonight—here—is the right time?"

"I couldn't wait any longer, Julian. Look, it's not the most terrible thing in the world. We'll just have to make the best of it."

"Are you insane?" Julian snarled. "There is no *best* of it!"

"Julian—"

"Do you really think I'm stupid enough to believe your lies? I know what you're up to, and I intend to have a word with a certain party. I might even speak to the boss."

"Julian, listen to me. You don't know what you're saying. You're just scared. But I promise you it'll be OK. Your life will hardly change at all. I'll make sure of it."

"No, you listen to me, Raylene." He lowered his voice and hissed something more that Tess could not make out.

Raylene's reaction was a shocked "*What*?"

"You heard me."

Raylene started to cry. "I don't believe you. If it were true, you'd have told me long before now."

"There was no point. I never expected anything like *this* to come up. I thought I made that very clear before we married."

"We're not the first couple—"

"Get out of here," he barked.

"I will not—"

"Go home and start packing. I want you to leave my house by the end of the week."

"It's my house, too!"

"We'll let the lawyers settle that. Until then, I want you out of my sight."

"*You* want! You want, Julian? What about what I want? I'm not going anywhere! If anybody moves out, it'll be you!"

"Not on your life. You'll go if I have to throw you out bodily."

"If you do, I will call the police. Don't think I won't, Julian," Raylene cried. Her voice rose a notch. "Stop it! You're hurting me!"

"You make me sick! Get away from me!"

There was a thump. Tess and Cinny exchanged alarmed looks and rushed up the stairs. By the time they got to the top, Julian was leaving by the door that led outside. Raylene was slumped against the wall where Julian must have shoved her, causing the thump they'd heard. She was still sobbing.

Tess placed her hand on Raylene's shoulder. "Are you all right?"

Her eyes were red and swollen. She clutched the wall for support. "I—I thought you'd left. Are you following me?"

"Of course not," Tess said. "We had to take the dirty linen down to the basement before we left. We couldn't help hearing you say that your husband was hurting you." Tess hoped Raylene would assume that's *all* they'd overheard.

"Oh, God," Raylene cried. "I don't know what I'm going to do." Then she seemed to catch herself, straightened, and shrugged off Tess's hand. "I—I'm fine. I have to go." She ran down the hall, brushing past Dahlia, who'd come out of the kitchen.

Cinny looked at Tess. "Oh, she's perfectly fine. Right."

"What's going on out here?" Dahlia asked.

"Julian and Raylene had an argument," Cinny said. "He went outside." She pointed to the door by which the chef had exited.

"That's it," Dahlia stated. "Bringing their domestic problems into the club is too much. Julian's behavior all evening has been beyond the pale." She went to the door and opened it. "I'm going to have a word with the man. And this time I'm laying down the law."

"Aunt Dahlia," Tess said, "I wouldn't try to talk to him right now. He's very upset."

"All the more reason to do it now, before he causes more trouble." Dahlia left, and Cinny and Tess went to the kitchen. Gertie was wiping countertops with a damp cloth. She made a final swipe and draped the cloth over a towel rack. "We're done here," she said with a sigh.

"Go home and get some rest," Tess said.

"We have to straighten things in the dining room before we can go home," Gertie told her. "I don't want to give that man anything to complain to his boss about."

Cinny and Tess followed her into the other room. "Where's your aunt, Tess?" Gertie asked. "When I came out of the pantry, she'd left the kitchen. I thought she'd come over here."

"She's looking for Julian," Tess said. Evidently Gertie

hadn't heard the Walkers' voices from the hall.

"She said she was going to lay down the law," Cinny said, chuckling. "Believe me, she can do it, too. I almost feel sorry for Julian—but not quite."

"Well, let's get these tables arranged," Gertie said. "I want to get out of here."

In fifteen minutes, the three women had set the dining room to rights. They sat down to wait for Dahlia's return.

"My feet hurt," Cinny complained, pulling off her high heels and wiggling her toes.

"If I took my shoes off," Gertie said, "I'd never get them back on." Several more minutes passed, and Gertie sat up suddenly. "Oh, I left my apron in the kitchen. I'll be right back."

When Gertie had not returned after a few minutes, Tess wondered if Julian was back in the kitchen harassing her again. "What do you suppose is keeping Gertie?"

Cinny had slumped down in her chair far enough to rest her head on the back. "She probably found something else to clean," she murmured.

After a while, Dahlia came back, looking totally frustrated. "I couldn't find Julian. Several of the people who came for the barbecue were still here, and I saw his wife getting in her car alone. Nobody seemed to know where Julian was. I guess he's gone home."

"Then let's do the same," Cinny said, sitting up and putting her shoes back on. "I'm bushed."

"I'm still going to give Julian Walker a piece of my mind the next time I see him," Dahlia proclaimed. "I may even speak to the board about his unforgivable behavior this evening."

"I can't imagine how Paula Overton will be able to stand working for him another eight months," Tess observed.

"From what I heard, she may not have the opportunity," Cinny said. "I think he really means to fire her."

"Aunt Dahlia, maybe you could speak to the board about

that, too," Tess said. "Tell them Paula is doing a good job and Julian has no grounds to let her go."

"I'll do that," Dahlia said.

"I'm out of here," Tess said. She wondered briefly if she should check on Gertie, but decided that she was being overly anxious. And she longed to fall into bed; she was so incredibly tired. Of course, she couldn't really retire until her family arrived, but she could get into her nightgown and robe and relax on the couch.

Gertie had driven her own car to the club, so Tess headed straight for the side entrance, near where she'd parked her car.

She heard a door closing somewhere, then hurried footsteps. She ignored the sounds. They had nothing to do with her.

Tess was half-out the exit door when she heard a garbled, almost-choking sound. She turned back. Dahlia and Cinny, who were partway down the hall behind Tess, halted, too, and looked toward the kitchen.

"What was that?" Cinny asked.

Dahlia took a step back. "Gertie?" she called.

After a moment, Gertie appeared in the kitchen doorway. Dropping the apron she held in her left hand, she gripped the door facing. Her face was so white she looked as if she needed the door frame to stay upright.

"Gertie!" Tess cried.

"I—it's—oh, my God," Gertie croaked.

Tess started back down the hall. Julian must have returned to the kitchen. She could think of nothing else that could have gotten Gertie so rattled. What in the world had the chef done now? It could be anything, considering the state he was in when he left his wife.

Gertie slumped against the door facing. "Help—me."

As Tess, Dahlia, and Cinny ran toward her, Tess saw something red on Gertie's right hand. Gertie lifted the hand and stared at it as if it were a foreign object she was amazed to see attached to her arm. Then Gertie made a gagging sound and swiped the hand down the front of her new pink dress, leaving a long stain.

Just as Tess reached her, Gertie moaned and slid slowly down until she sat, crumpled like a rag doll against the door facing.

Chapter 6

"Good heavens, you've cut yourself," Dahlia exclaimed as she bent over Gertie's slumped form. "Get me a wet cloth, Cinny."

Cinny hurried into the kitchen, returning with a dish towel that she'd wet on one end.

Dahlia took it and began wiping Gertie's hand. "I can't see where it's coming from," she said finally. "Where did you cut yourself, Gertie?"

Gertie swallowed hard and shook her head. "No." She shot a terrified glance over her shoulder. "I didn't cut myself."

"But what—"

"Look—" Gertie gasped. "The pantry."

Tess walked to the pantry door and Cinny followed her. Behind them, Tess heard Dahlia say, "I'm so sorry you were treated badly this evening, Gertie. If that man touched you . . . Can you stand up? Here, let me help you."

Tess pushed against the door, but it would open only halfway. It had hit something solid, perhaps a large food can that had been used as a door stop. She squeezed around the edge of the swinging door.

It wasn't a can of food. Tess comprehended that at the same moment her stomach lurched upward.

Julian Walker half-lay, half-sat with his back against shelves of canned goods and sacks of flour, sugar, and cornmeal. That he was dead was made clear by his wide, unfocused eyes, the butcher knife protruding from his chest, and the blood that had soaked the front of his white shirt.

Cinny pressed in against Tess's back, craning to see over Tess's shoulder. "Oh, my Lord," she gasped.

Tess took one step toward the body, feeling suddenly as if she were encased in ice. When she could breathe again and truly believe what she saw, she realized that they were contaminating a crime scene. She backed up and said in a thin but controlled voice, "Cinny, call the police."

Police Chief Desmond Butts and Officer Andy Neill arrived within the quarter-hour. Other people still at the country club had been rounded up and sent to the dining room. They were now waiting for Butts and Neill to finish securing the crime scene.

Tess's Uncle Maurice, Dahlia's husband, had come in looking for his wife as Cinny was phoning the police station. A banker accustomed to directing thirty-some employees, he immediately took charge of the situation; made certain Dahlia, Cinny, Tess, and Gertie were all right; and made a circuit of the club and grounds, telling whomever he saw that they had a "situation," the police were expected momentarily, and they should all wait in the dining room.

Maurice Forrest was a tall, imposing man who, from appearance and demeanor, might have been an international business tycoon or an important player on Wall Street instead of a small-town banker. As witness to his authoritative manner, nobody had thought to object to being detained by him.

Returning from making a quick circuit of the grounds, Maurice caught Tess in the hallway. "You OK, honey?"

She nodded, and he patted her shoulder comfortingly. "I'm so sorry this had to happen on the night of your shower."

Tess sighed. "Thanks, Uncle Maurice. At least on another night, Gertie wouldn't have been here to discover the body."

Frowning, he glanced beyond Tess down the hallway. "Dahlia is sitting with Gertie. I didn't see Wayne or Jed on the patio. Would you check and see if they're in Jed's office? I better go in and try to keep everybody calm."

Tess made her way through the reception area to the office suite beyond. She heard voices from behind the closed door of the manager's office.

"We should make a decision next week sometime."

"It seems to make little difference to the architect which site we choose. He says either would be quite workable." Tess recognized the second voice as that of the manager, Jed Baskin.

"Maybe, but I'm inclined to listen to Linzy. He should know better than anyone which site best suits our needs."

"Whichever choice the board makes, it will be none too soon. Johnny is having trouble scheduling tee times, fitting everybody in, especially on weekends. Our membership has grown so fast the past couple of years."

"More members, more membership fees. And we're going to need them to buy that land."

"True, but we're getting people from all over the county now," Jed said.

"With the new course, we'll be even more attractive to them."

"Maybe we should postpone considering any additional membership applications until the new course is finished."

Tess tapped on the door.

There was movement in the office, and Jed Baskin opened the door. He frowned and peered over her shoulder. "I guess Kaylynn left. Dammit, she knew I wanted her to answer the phone till I'm ready to leave." Tess surmised that Kaylynn was the new girl, the one Dahlia had described as "scattered." Baskin, a short, wiry man in his forties, was full of nervous energy and massaged the side of his neck with one hand as though working out a kinked muscle.

"Sorry, Tess," Baskin went on. "Did everything go all right with your shower?"

"The shower was wonderful. Jed, I hate to disturb you, but something's happened . . ."

Wayne Trammell, chairman of the governing board, rose from the leather sofa in the office. A thick, beefy man, he wore shorts and a shirt imprinted with the club logo. "Come on in, Tess. This isn't a private meeting. We were just discussing the club's growing pains. It's a nice problem to have, but still a problem."

Tess stepped into the office. Jed's tired but expectant expression made her hate to break the news of the murder. Poor Jed would have to deal with the reporters. She hoped nobody but the local newspaper and perhaps the Springfield media would be interested in running a story. After all, Julian was not a public figure.

Perhaps sensing Tess's reluctance to speak, Wayne said, "I understand Frank will be in sometime tonight."

"In a couple of hours."

"Can't wait to see my old buddy. With Oliver here, too, it'll be like old times."

"I know Dad's looking forward to it," Tess said.

"Tess, if the chef gave you any more problems—" Jed began.

Tess shook her head, wishing Julian's continued unacceptable behavior was the only thing she had to report. "It's not that. It's . . . Julian is dead—murdered."

Both men stared at her. Jed ran a hand over his perpetual five o'clock shadow, then gripped his desk, as if to keep himself from staggering. Wayne, a successful businessman in his late fifties, whose gray hair had receded to the middle of his crown, sat down suddenly on the couch. The news had made his legs weak.

"You did say murdered, didn't you, Tess?" Wayne queried, passing a hand across the top of his head, as if searching for his vanished hair.

"He was stabbed," Tess said, "in the pantry. My cook, Gertie Bogart, found him. The police have arrived, and Chief Butts wants to see everybody in the big dining room."

"Julian spoke to me about Mrs. Bogart earlier," Jed said. "He wanted me to ask her to leave the club."

"What happened?" Wayne inserted. "I know Mrs. Bogart and Julian had some kind of blow-up. Did Julian threaten her physically? Because if he did, that's extenuating circumstances and—"

"No!" Tess said. It sounded as if Wayne had jumped to the conclusion that Gertie had killed the chef. How many other people knew about the trouble between Julian and Gertie and would harbor the same suspicion? She must put a stop to any such notion at once. "Gertie found the body, Wayne. She had nothing to do with Julian's death."

Wayne and Jed exchanged a look. "Of course . . ." Wayne murmured, not sounding totally convinced of Gertie's innocence.

"We'd better not keep Chief Butts waiting any longer," Jed said, and the two men followed Tess to the dining room.

Trammell and Baskin joined golf pro Johnny Linzy and his wife, Wendy, at one of the tables. "Can you believe this?" Johnny greeted the newcomers. "We were getting into our car when Maurice Forrest flagged us down."

Chief Butts cleared his throat portentously. "Is anybody else still around?"

Maurice spoke up. "I think this is everybody, Chief."

Tess glanced around the room. Paula Overton sat with the two young men hired to help with the barbecue. They'd been brought in from the patio, where they'd been doing the final clean-up.

Gertie, who sat at a table with Dahlia and Maurice, was talking very little, answering Dahlia's soft, solicitous questions with monosyllables. Tess suspected that Dahlia was trying to learn if Gertie had heard or seen anything suspicious in the kitchen during the evening. Gertie just kept shaking her head.

"In case any of you don't know why we're here," Butts said, "Julian Walker, your chef, has been stabbed—in the pantry. A nasty way to die."

Tess studied faces. Jed Baskin gazed at Butts for a long moment, then turned to look at Wayne Trammell, who'd bowed his head, as if in deference to the dead. Jed mumbled something to his tablemates. Trammell shook his head to whatever Baskin said.

Wendy Linzy gripped her husband's hand, her face pale beneath the tan. Johnny's mouth was set in a hard line, and he turned to exchange an uneasy look with his wife. Wendy leaned toward him and whispered urgently. He frowned and shushed her.

Paula Overton had merely bowed her head, not looking at anyone. She'd removed her hairnet, and her straight brown hair had fallen forward so that Tess couldn't see her face.

The two high school boys appeared to be truly stunned. Perhaps they'd been wondering what hit them ever since Julian had raked them over the coals earlier. Tess suspected they were wishing they'd never set foot in the country club.

If Tess had hoped to find guilt written on one of the faces in the room, she was disappointed. She wondered how Raylene Walker might have reacted, but the chef's wife had evidently already left the club while Maurice was gathering up the stragglers.

Chief Butts scanned the room, finally acknowledging Tess with a nod. "So, Tess," he growled, "I didn't expect to find you here. Call me a cock-eyed optimist." The others turned to stare curiously at Tess. Butts did not seem to expect a reply, so she made none. What could she say? She *had* been involved in several homicide investigations, through no fault of her own. She put it down to bad luck.

Then Butts questioned everyone briefly. Where had they been in the thirty minutes before the body was discovered? Could anyone vouch for their alibis? Butts use of the word "alibi" raised some eyebrows. The chief continued with his questions. Who else had been at the club during that half-hour? Did anybody know of Julian Walker's having a confrontation with another person during the evening?

When no one responded immediately to the last question, Dahlia said, "Julian was in a foul mood all night. I wouldn't be surprised if he had words with several people."

Butts lifted his bushy eyebrows above the metal rims of his eyeglasses. "What was he in a foul mood about?"

Dahlia glanced at Tess before she said, "For one thing, he didn't like the idea that we'd brought in food from outside for Tess's bridal shower. He didn't want us using the kitchen, and when we insisted, he went to complain to Jed Baskin about it."

Jed nodded. "I told him Mrs. Forrest had cleared it with me and that he was to let the women make their preparations."

"How did Walker react to that?" Butts asked.

"He wasn't happy about it," Jed replied, "but he didn't have to be happy. He just had to follow instructions. I'm his boss."

Butts glanced at Tess. "Did he give you any more problems?"

Tess shrugged. "He continued to be unpleasant, not just to me and Gertie and Cinny and Aunt Dahlia, but to Paula and those two young men who were helping with the barbecue."

Paula's head came up at the mention of her name. She looked as if she'd like to melt into the teal-colored carpet.

"Miss Overton?" Butts said, "you're Walker's assistant, right?"

"I'm doing a year's training under him to finish the requirements for certification by COA. That's Chefs of America. Its members include the most highly regarded chefs in the country."

Butts waved her explanation aside. "Yeah, yeah. So how did you and Walker get along?"

She glanced toward Tess and Cinny. "All right, I guess. I mean, I got along with him about as well as anybody else did. Julian had a temper, and sometimes he lashed out at whoever happened to be handy."

"And you were usually handy," Butts mumbled.

"Sometimes," Paula said softly.

Both of the teenage boys were well-muscled, as if they were into weight-lifting. One of them spoke up. "I was only hired for this one night, but Mr. Walker was impossible to get along with. He yelled at Craig and me"—he glanced at the other young man—"for being a few minutes late. I told him we had a flat, but he didn't care, said we'd never work here again."

"That was OK by us," the other boy put in. "*I* sure didn't want to work for him again. I don't see how Paula took it. Tonight he even threatened to fire her." He seemed to know Paula, and Tess remembered that she'd been the one who had hired the boys, another thing for which she'd been criticized by Julian Walker.

Paula sank down in her chair, still trying to disappear. Butts gazed at her. "Did he now? That wouldn't look too good on your record, would it, Miss Overton?"

"Julian threatened to fire me all the time," Paula protested.

"Maybe this time he meant it," Butts said.

She shook her head. "No, he wouldn't have done it."

"But how could you know for sure?" Butts inquired. Before Paula could reply, he went on, "Anybody else have a problem with Walker tonight, or see anyone who did?"

Cinny elbowed Tess and Tess cleared her throat. "Cinny and I overheard Julian and his wife having a terrible argument—it must have been forty-five minutes or so before Gertie found the body. He told her to go home and pack her things, he wanted her out of the house. He pushed her against the wall. She was crying when he left her."

Butts made another note in his pocket-sized spiral notebook. "OK, anybody else have anything to tell me?"

Nobody spoke.

Tess glanced furtively in Gertie's direction, but Gertie had her head down, as though trying to distance herself from the entire proceeding.

Butts got everyone's name, address, and phone number. "Before you leave, Officer Neill will take your fingerprints in that room next to the kitchen."

"Fingerprints?" blurted Jed Baskin. "What for?"

"In case we find prints on the murder weapon," Butts told him.

"Surely you don't suspect it was one of us who killed Julian," Baskin blustered.

"Far as I can tell, you were the only ones here."

"There were several other people around when Jed and I went into his office about twenty minutes ago," Wayne Trammell put in.

"I know the chef's wife was here," Butts asked. "I'll need the names of the others as soon as we finish. If anybody else thinks of anything—anything at all—that might bear on this case, contact me right away. Now, all of you can go in to Officer Neill for the fingerprinting. Give me those names now, Mr. Trammell. Miz Bogart, I'll need a word with you before you go."

Tess waited in the hall with Wayne Trammell while Butts grilled Gertie; there was no other word for it. Gertie admitted, without elaborating, to having words with Julian during the evening. When Butts pressed her for details, she only said that he didn't like having strangers in his kitchen, especially another cook. Butts continued to press, sounding as though he doubted her version of events. Tess did not like the way things were going.

"How'd you get that stain on your dress?" Butts asked.

"When I found him, I—I reached down without thinking to touch him and see if he was alive. It was obvious he wasn't, but I too shocked to think straight."

"Yeah?" Butts inquired heavily.

"I got blood on my hand and wiped it on my dress." She glanced down at the stain. "Probably ruined it, but as I said, I wasn't thinking."

Butts remained noncommittal, but his eyes were suspiciously speculative.

Trammell leaned toward Tess and mumbled, "Maybe Jed's right, we're taking in new people too fast. We don't know enough about some of them. Maybe we should do better background checks. For all we know, we've accepted somebody with a criminal record."

Tess nodded abstractedly, her attention still on Gertie and Butts. She didn't bother pointing out that everybody still at the club was either an employee or a long-time member. Wayne was grasping for an explanation. "Thank God my wife left before all this. It's just the kind of situation in which Esther likes to throw her weight around." Esther Trammell was known around the club for being very demanding.

"She'll probably have to talk to the police sooner or later," Tess said. "I imagine Chief Butts will eventually talk to everyone who was here tonight."

Wayne accepted this probability with a heavy sigh.

When Butts finally let Gertie go, Wayne asked her if she was all right. Gertie said she was, and Wayne went to the green room to have his fingerprints taken. Tess hugged Gertie, and they followed Wayne.

Afterward, Tess told Gertie to go home and take the next day off if she wanted to, even though that meant Tess would have to prepare breakfast for her guests.

"No, I'll be at Iris House in the morning, same as usual,

Tess. I'd rather be working, keeps my mind occupied." She started to say something else, but Butts came out of the kitchen just then. Gertie hurried away.

"There's something else I want to tell you, Chief," Tess said. "I didn't want to mention it in front of the others."

Butts studied her with a faintly befuddled expression. "Go ahead."

"Before Raylene Walker and her husband had that argument, she and another man argued. I was in the dining room, and they were at the end of the hall." She pointed to the spot.

"Who was this other man?"

"I don't know, but I'm sure it wasn't Julian. When I looked out, he was gone and Raylene was crying."

"Sounds like Raylene Walker spent the evening crying, and you spent the evening listening to other people's conversations."

"My overhearing Raylene and the men was mere coincidence."

Butts nodded, looking somewhat amused. "Tell you what, Tess. Why don't you write down everything you can remember about those two arguments. Everything Raylene Walker said and what her husband and the other man said."

"I'm getting married in two weeks, Chief. I still have lots to do. But I'll get to it as soon as possible."

Butts was clearly not impressed by her full schedule. "I'll need it tomorrow morning, Tess. I'll be by at ten to pick up your statement." He walked toward the kitchen, and Tess, at long last, headed home.

Leaving the air-conditioned building was like walking into a sauna, but a soft, welcome breeze coming from the south made it tolerable. Tess walked tiredly toward her car and saw that Gertie's car was still parked beside Tess's. As Tess reached her car, Gertie's driver-side window slid down and she called Tess over.

"Are you OK?" Tess asked.

"Yes, but I kept some things back when I was talking to Chief Butts," Gertie said.

"I know. I heard you and Julian arguing in the pantry. Remember? You knew him before, didn't you? Something happened between you and Julian two years ago."

Gertie's face was in shadow, and Tess couldn't see her expression, but she saw Gertie's nod. "We were both contestants in a cooking competition in New York City. The best chefs in the country were there—and somehow I got invited. I was ahead in points until the last day. Julian won by sabotaging me."

Tess lifted her hair off the back of her neck to let the breeze cool it. "I don't understand, Gertie. How did he sabotage you?"

She sighed heavily. "I don't want to go into it now, Tess." Her voice quivered. "It'll probably sound silly, except that there was a big money prize at stake. I'm just wondering if I should tell Chief Butts about it."

"I would if I were you."

"It'll look like I had a motive to kill him, and with me finding the body and all . . . I didn't do it, Tess."

"Oh, of course, you didn't. I never thought for a moment that you did, Gertie."

"And you still think I should tell the chief about it?"

"If you don't, and he finds out some other way, it will look even worse for you."

She slumped forward over the wheel. "I guess I knew that already. I was just trying to find a way to get around it—hoping you'd convince me it's OK to keep quiet."

"Sorry, but Chief Butts will talk to Julian's wife. If Butts brings up your name, Raylene could recognize it."

"And she'll tell him about the trouble in New York."

"Yes. It's better if you tell him first."

Gertie bowed her head and made little sniffing sounds. She was crying. Tess reached through the open window and patted her shoulder. "It'll be all right, Gertie. Julian and his wife were having marital problems. He told her to pack her things tonight and leave. She has no job and may have nowhere else to go. Raylene Walker is a much more likely suspect than you."

Gertie wiped her eyes with the back of her hand. "I guess Paula Overton could be considered a suspect, too, even though I can't imagine that mousy little thing hurting a fly."

"People do unbelievable things when backed into a corner, Gertie," Tess said. "Paula said herself that if she lost this apprenticeship she'd have a hard time finding another. And she probably wouldn't get her certificate or whatever they get at chef's school. If Julian had actually fired her, he would undoubtedly have blackballed her, too."

"I don't have a certificate, either, and I've done all right. But it would be like Julian Walker to blackball Paula," Gertie observed. "He is—was—such a vindictive man."

"Try not to say things like that to the police," Tess cautioned. "Just give them the facts."

"OK, Tess, I'll go to the police station tomorrow and tell Chief Butts everything."

"You won't have to go there. I overheard Julian and Raylene arguing. She also argued with another man earlier. Butts asked me to write down everything I could remember about those conversations. He's coming to Iris House in the morning to get my statement. You can speak to him then."

Gertie peered up at Tess from the dimness of her car. "Will you stay with me when I do it?"

"Of course. Now go home and try to get some rest."

Gertie drove away, and Tess got into her car and started the engine. She would be surprised if Gertie managed to get any sleep at all tonight. Tess herself would do well to get in a couple of hours. First, she had to go home and wait up for her family. Since sleep would be elusive, she could spend the time putting away the gifts.

Chapter 7

In her dream, Wendy Linzy was searching her house desperately for her husband and son. Driving her frantic search was the feeling that something was wrong, terribly wrong. Johnny and Marcus were in danger, and she had to find them before . . .

Before what?

She was not to know because she came awake with a start, her heart pumping fearfully. Her nightgown was damp with perspiration. Pushing her dark hair off her face, she saw that the digital clock beside the bed read 1:15. Shaking the last shreds of her dream away, she lay back down and reached for the comfort of her husband's body.

Johnny wasn't there.

She sat up again. "Johnny?"

There was no answer. She swung her feet over the side of the bed, switched on a lamp, and glanced toward the bathroom. In the moonlight drifting through the windows, she could see that the bathroom door was open but the light wasn't on. Johnny had probably gone downstairs as soon as she was asleep to keep from disturbing her. He hadn't been sleeping well lately, he hadn't been himself in other ways, either. Something heavy weighed on his mind, something he refused to talk to her about.

But after what they'd been through tonight at the club, it was not surprising he couldn't sleep. Johnny and Julian Walker hadn't been friends, but Julian *had* been a coworker, and Johnny had been shaken by the news of Julian's murder, so shaken, in fact, that he'd asked Wendy to drive them home.

She left the master bedroom, paused at Marcus's room to check on him. Her son was sprawled on his stomach, stuffed animals—most of them gifts from his grandfather—piled around him, fast asleep. As she bent over his bed to pull the tangled sheet across his legs, her heart swelled with maternal love.

Leaving the door of her son's room slightly ajar, she descended the stairs and turned toward the kitchen, where the light streamed through the doorway and into the dining room, which she'd furnished with country French antiques. In contrast, the kitchen was a white-and-black model of modern appliances and gadgets. She usually cast an admiring glance about whenever she passed through the rooms of her house, but at the moment she was fully occupied with finding out what was wrong with her husband.

Johnny was standing at the patio doors in the jockey shorts he wore to sleep because he said pajamas were too confining. She stood still and watched him in silence for an instant, the only man she'd ever loved, except for her father. He stared out at the backyard, which was dimly illuminated by a couple of yard lamps.

Anxiety trickled through her. They argued too often these days, usually about money. She wished he wouldn't take things so seriously.

"Honey?" Wendy said softly.

He turned around. "I didn't hear you, Wen. I'm sorry if I woke you."

"You didn't. I was having a bad dream."

His mouth curled in an ironic smile. "I didn't know you ever had bad dreams, sunshine."

He had given her that name when they were dating. He had said just seeing her face always gave him a lift, that it was like the sun breaking through a cloudy sky. But he hadn't called her that in months. Hearing him say it now helped ease the tension that had been with her since they'd left the club last night. She'd made several efforts to start a conversation on the short drive home, but he'd responded only with grunts, so she'd finally given up.

She moved to his side and took his hand. "Trouble sleeping?"

"Yeah."

"It's no wonder. Poor Julian. I didn't care for the man, but the way he died—" She shuddered.

"It was terrible," he agreed, "but it's not just that."

She studied his handsome profile. "Are you really afraid of losing your job?"

He shrugged.

"Johnny, you know Daddy is more than willing to help us, if it comes to that."

He disentangled his fingers from hers. "Your father has helped us too much already," he said shortly. "Besides, we'd have something saved if you didn't spend money like it was going out of style."

They'd had this discussion before—too many times. "I'm not half as extravagant as some of my friends."

"Most of your friends' husbands make more than I do. But you think you have to go shopping whenever they ask. Sometimes I think it's a competition with you, to see who can spend the most."

"That's not true, Johnny, but I need to get out of the house occasionally."

"I don't mind your getting out of the house, but you always come home from those outings with new clothes you don't need. There have been clothes in your closet for weeks that you haven't even gotten around to wearing yet. You behave just as you did before we were married, when your father was paying the bills."

"Sweetheart, Daddy *wants* to make our life easier. I'll get his money eventually, anyway. Why not let him be generous while he's still around to enjoy it?"

Losing his grip on his temper, he grabbed her upper arms and jerked her closer to him. "What he enjoys is humiliating me! You are not to ask your father for more money, Wendy. Understand?"

She stared at him in amazement. Why was he so angry with her? Oh, they had their differences about her spending habits, but she'd always managed to get around him before.

"Let me go, Johnny."

He released her abruptly and turned away.

"Don't ever touch me in anger again. As much as I love you, I won't stand for that, Johnny."

He expelled a long breath. "Can't you understand how worthless it makes me feel when you go to your father for money?"

"I'm sorry about that, but I'm not responsible for your feelings. I swear you'd find something to feel worthless about if it wasn't the money. I know your father never had a good word to say for you, but you're a grown man now, Johnny. Isn't it time you got over it?"

He turned back to her, anger still smoldering in his eyes. "I can provide for my family—maybe not in the way you were accustomed to before we married. But we can live comfortably if you'll stop throwing money out the window. I don't want your father's money! Promise me you will not ask him again."

She promised because he was so upset, even though she knew she would probably take more money from her father. She didn't have to ask outright. All she had to do was mention there was something she wanted for the house or for Marcus that they couldn't afford on Johnny's salary.

Chapter 8

In spite of her anxiety over the meeting with Chief Butts, Gertie did herself proud with the next morning's breakfast, a buffet of eggs scrambled with minced onion and pimento, gravy, biscuits, pancakes, cinnamon rolls, sausage links, bacon, fresh fruit, and fruit juice. The spread would have fed a crew of farm laborers.

Tess's family—her father, Frank; stepmother, Zelda; fifteen-year-old half-sister, Madison; and fourteen-year-old half-brother, Curt—had arrived a few minutes after one A.M. They'd all stayed up to talk. Tess gave them the details of the shower and the evening's grand finale, the discovery of the chef's murdered body. Of course, that elicited a barrage of questions, which she answered as best she could. Murder at a bridal shower? Unbelievable, according to her father, even though Tess kept saying that the chef really hadn't been involved in the shower. That the murder occurred on that particular night was mere coincidence.

Finally, they were all too exhausted to talk anymore, and Tess showed her father and Zelda upstairs to the Darcy Flame Suite. Madison was installed in the Carnaby Room and Curt in the Black Swan Room.

Except for the Stedmans in the Anabel Jane Room,

Iris House was closed to outsiders until after the wedding. So that Tess wouldn't have to cancel the reservations for the two weeks following the wedding, Gertie had agreed to stay in Tess and Luke's quarters while they were on their honeymoon. Where she and Luke were going was still a mystery to Tess. Luke insisted on keeping their destination a secret.

By three A.M., when she finally retired, Tess was so wound up she couldn't fall asleep for another half-hour. She kept seeing Julian Walker's bloody body with the butcher knife sticking out of his chest, kept replaying the arguments and run-ins Julian had had with various people during the evening. Was there a clue somewhere in all of that which would identify the killer? If so, she didn't find it.

At nine A.M., she'd dragged herself into the guest dining room to find her family and the Stedmans already at breakfast.

Ruth Stedman, a small, sweet-faced woman, gave Tess a sympathetic smile. "You poor dear," she commiserated in her soft voice. "Did you get a wink of sleep last night after your terrible ordeal?" Plainly, her family had already told the Stedmans about the chef's murder at the country club.

"A few," Tess said as she poured herself a cup of coffee from the buffet.

"Wayne has already called to tell me the police will probably want to talk to me," Oliver Stedman said. "It seems they're talking to anybody who was there until shortly before the body was discovered, and that includes me. After the barbecue, I met with Wayne and the golf pro about that land of mine the club is interested in."

"When you left, I don't suppose you noticed anybody acting suspicious," Tess said.

"Suspicious, how?"

"Somebody coming out of the kitchen or the small dining room. Both rooms have doors into the pantry, where the chef's body was found. Or maybe you saw somebody leaving the club in a hurry."

"Sorry, no," Stedman said.

Tess sighed. "Well, Chief Butts is coming here this morning at ten. He'll probably want to talk to you then."

"I'll be on the golf course," Oliver said. "He can run me down later."

"Oliver," Frank said, "do you know yet if they're going to buy your land?"

"It's looking very promising," Oliver said. "The board will take a final vote in a few days. I'm keeping my fingers crossed."

Ruth laughed softly. "I objected to Oliver's buying that land fifteen years ago. It was just an old, worn-out farm. The farmhouse wasn't even worth fixing up. He kept saying it would pay off one day and, mercy, he was right—if the country club buys it, that is."

"I'm looking forward to seeing old Wayne again," Frank said. "It's been at least ten years."

"He hasn't changed much," Oliver told him. "Put on a few more pounds maybe—like the rest of us." He patted his stomach.

"How's Esther?" Frank asked.

"She had a headache and left the barbecue early," Oliver replied. "Later, Wayne mentioned that she was after him to buy some new clothes and that he would probably have to let her take him shopping after our golf game today."

Frank laughed. "Same old Wayne. He still hates shopping."

"Don't all men?" Zelda queried.

"Yeah, but Wayne hates it even more than most of us," Frank told her. "He used to buy two or three identical shirts or pants, when he found some he liked, just to keep from going shopping again for a long time."

"I'm sure he still does it," Oliver added. "And apparently Esther still nags him about his wardrobe."

Tess carried her coffee to the table and sat beside her father, who put down his fork to give her a hug.

"Why don't you take the day off to relax, honey?" he

asked. "I think the rest of us will probably take a nap this afternoon."

"I have too much to do, Daddy."

"Could I do some of it for you?" Zelda offered. She was a stout-looking woman—not overweight, but big-boned—with prematurely gray hair which she made no effort to hide with color or frosting. Tess had always thought Zelda gave off an aura of extreme competence. She was good-hearted, if a bit opinionated at times. Tess had resented Zelda when her father married her. She'd seen Zelda as an interloper trying to take her late mother's place. A natural reaction for a fourteen-year-old, she supposed. But in the years since, she'd come to like Zelda, and she adored Madison and Curt. After all, Zelda had to have something going for her to have raised two such great kids.

"That's sweet of you, Zelda," Tess said. "Are you really sure you want to?"

"Positive," Zelda told her.

"Let me think. You could run by the jeweler's and pick up Luke's ring and stop at the stationer's on the way. The napkins for the reception should be ready. If it isn't too much trouble, that is. I know this is a holiday for you."

Zelda waved away Tess's words. "Consider it done. Just write down the addresses for me. Your father and Oliver are going golfing with Wayne Trammell, so Ruth and the kids and I plan to do a little shopping in town. It'll be no trouble at all."

"We'll help, too, Tess," Curt inserted. He was as good-humored, as skinny and freckled as he'd been last Christmas, the last time she'd seen him, but he must have grown another two or three inches. He was going to top six feet before he attained his full adult height.

"Is my maid-of-honor dress ready, do you think?" asked Madison, already a dark-haired beauty at fifteen. She would be stunning in the yellow silk dress Tess had chosen for her.

"Almost," Tess said. "I'll call the seamstress later today

and see if I can take you for a final fitting. Curt, Luke is taking care of the tuxedos, although you may have to go and be measured. I swear you've grown since your mother sent me your measurements." Curt would be a groomsman at the wedding.

"He's gone through three sizes of jeans already this year," Zelda said. "Seems every time he puts on a pair, they're too short."

"I'm two inches taller than Maddie now," Curt said, grinning at his sister.

Madison stuck out her tongue. "Don't let it go to your head, little brother. No matter how tall you get, I'll always be older than you."

"Yeah, when you're forty, I'll still be in my thirties."

"Oh, go fall out of a tree or something." Although she wanted to be considered a young woman, Madison was still kid enough to let her brother's teasing get under her skin. Now she turned back to Tess. "Maybe I could help you put up your shower gifts, Tess."

"I'd really appreciate that. I meant to take care of it last night, while I waited for you all, but I was so tired I couldn't make myself do it." Tess looked around the table. "Thank you all so much for wanting to help." Unexpectedly, Tess's eyes grew a little moist. She blinked to clear her vision. "I'm so glad to have my family here."

"We're glad to be here, too, sweetie, and we'll do whatever we can to help," her father assured her. "So don't worry."

"I'll try," Tess said. "Now, as soon as I eat breakfast, I have to get my statement ready for Chief Butts. Later today, I'll try to figure out what to do about the food for the reception. Julian Walker was supposed to be in charge of that. I only hope his assistant can take over."

Gertie thrust her head out of the kitchen. "If she can't, I can."

"Thanks, Gertie, but putting more work on you is an absolute last resort. You have enough to do without that."

Not the least of which, Tess feared, was to convince Chief Butts she had nothing to do with Julian Walker's murder. But, no, she told herself, that was too ludicrous for even Chief Butts to credit. She was just overtired, and that was making her feel pessimistic. Maybe she could find time for a nap this afternoon herself.

Chapter 9

By mid-morning, everybody but Tess and Gertie had gone his separate way. Chief Butts arrived at ten on schedule. Tess had made three pages of notes on the two highly charged conversations she'd overheard Raylene Walker have with Julian and the still-unidentified second man. She handed them to the chief when he walked in.

Butts sat down heavily on the green velvet settee in the guest parlor and read through her statement while Gertie hovered near the archway between the parlor and the guest dining room and Tess waited quietly beside the lace-curtained front window. She was *outwardly* quiet, at any rate. Inside, her mind spun with all the things she needed to do later that day. She wished the chief would complete his business there and leave.

Butts finished reading and looked up at Tess. "Sounds like Miz Walker's had a personal relationship with this other man," he observed as he folded the sheets of paper together and stuffed them into his shirt pocket, "and her husband was sure mad at her about something. Maybe Walker suspected she'd been carrying on with the other guy." From another pocket, he removed a toothpick and stuck it between his teeth.

"He was certainly furious about something," Tess said, "but then so was the other man."

"Sounds like both these guys wanted her to disappear," Butts observed around the toothpick. "I'm surprised she wasn't the one who got stabbed." He pulled Tess's statement out again, unfolded it, and read a section. "The first man told her to deal with something and be discreet about it. What do you reckon that means?"

"I don't know, but Raylene said they had to deal with the problem together. If they'd been having an affair, for example, it might have meant that he wanted to end it and she didn't."

Butts removed the toothpick from his mouth. "She could've threatened to tell her husband—the other man's wife, even, if he's married."

"And Julian threatened to speak to his boss. That would be Jed Baskin. But I doubt Julian had time for that before he was killed. Still, why would he think Jed would be interested in his marital problems?"

"Can't say, but I sure would like to get this case wrapped up pronto. A murder at the country club is going to have the townsfolk pressuring me big time. I can hear 'em now— aren't we even safe in a private club? It's not like one of those homeless guys down by the tracks got done in." He sighed heavily. "I'll talk to Raylene Walker again, too. Maybe she'll tell me what all the fuss was about last night."

"Good luck, but I doubt she'll tell you anything personal."

"Yeah." Butts stuffed the notes and toothpick back in his pocket and planted both beefy hands on his thighs, his elbows pointing out. "I'm going out to the Walker house this afternoon. I'll try to intimidate her into coming clean."

"Don't count on it," Tess said. "The less you know about Raylene and Julian's marriage trouble, the better for Raylene. She was awfully upset after that conversation with Julian last night. But I'll bet she tries to play it down when you talk to her. She has to realize she's a suspect in the murder. An angry wife who's just been told to get out of the house couldn't help but think that her problem would be solved if her husband were suddenly not around anymore."

"She's on my suspect list, all right." He patted his pocket. "And she's not the only one."

Tess was relieved to hear that he was considering suspects other than Gertie, but she feared that when he heard about the problem with Julian Walker two years earlier, he'd turn the spotlight back again.

"You have to find out who the other man is," Tess said. "From what Julian said, I think he knew—or suspected—that Raylene was having an affair. The 'certain party' Julian said he'd have a word with must've been the lover. If Julian confronted him and the other man wanted to keep it quiet . . . well, Julian was angry enough not to care who heard him. He could even have threatened to name the other man in a divorce case. What if the man had good reasons not to want the story to get out? He could've felt killing Julian was the only way to keep him from talking."

Butts scratched the end of his nose, a crease forming above his eyeglasses between his brows. The chief had a face that would look at home on a wanted poster—a square jaw, wide nose, hard eyes, thick eyebrows, and hair as coarse and straight as a scrub brush's bristles.

"From what she said," Butts went on, "it sounds like Miz Walker had been carrying on with this other guy for quite a while. Somebody is bound to know about it." He pushed off the settee with his hands and hauled himself to his feet with a grunt. "Try to keep a secret around here, good luck. I can't even rent an R-rated video in this town without the word getting out." He darted a sharp look at Tess. "If you hear anything, let me know right away."

Tess nodded, remembering Dahlia's reference to Julian's "personal problem." As soon as she found time for a private talk with her aunt, she'd get that secret out of her. "Of course," she replied to Butts.

He walked across the parlor, and Tess glanced toward the dining room. Gertie gave her a questioning look. "Chief," Tess said, "Gertie has something to tell you before you go."

He turned back. "Say it's a confession. I'd like to get this case wrapped up today." He half-grinned, half-grimaced, and Tess wasn't sure whether he was joking or not. Butts's humor was rare and tended toward sarcasm.

Gertie came reluctantly into the parlor. "I didn't kill that man, Chief Butts."

Butts studied her for a moment. "Did you know, Miz Bogart, that ninety-nine percent of the murderers in the state penitentiary claim they're innocent?"

Again, Tess wondered if he was serious, comparing Gertie to the worst criminals behind bars.

"I didn't like the man," Gertie admitted, "but there are a few other people I don't like, either, and I've never considered killing any of them."

Butts snorted and pushed his eyeglasses up his nose with a thick index finger. "Damn, she ain't gonna confess, after all." He fished a small spiral tablet from the hip pocket of his khaki uniform and sat back down on the settee. "Say your piece, then."

Gertie slowly lowered herself onto the the edge of the floral chinz sofa, facing him. "I knew Julian Walker before."

Tess sat down beside her and patted her hand, wanting to reassure her. Butts flipped the cover on his tablet back and glanced up at Gertie with an interested expression. "Before he came to Victoria Springs?"

"Yes. Two years ago, I took part in a cooking contest in New York City. It was sponsored by a big food company."

"One of those bake-off things," Butts observed.

Gertie nodded. "One of the biggest, and the grand prize was fifty thousand dollars."

"What company did you say sponsored the contest?"

"Bowers and Leek. They have those ads on TV where a woman puts a pie in the oven and then starts singing and dancing and her husband comes in and catches her."

Butts looked impressed. "Yeah, I've seen those. You know, I might even put on an apron myself for a chance at that kind of money. Did you win?"

"No. Julian Walker did."

"Too bad." Butts gnawed the cap end of his ballpoint pen. "I guess that got your Irish up, your reputation as a cook and all, must've made you mighty jealous."

Gertie stiffened. "I wasn't jealous. I was furious! I should have come home with that money, and I would have if Julian Walker hadn't sabotaged me."

Butts cocked his head questioningly. "How'd he manage that, caught you using a cake mix or something?"

Clearly Gertie did not appreciate Butts's weak attempt at a joke. She looked disgusted. "He put salt in my sugar."

Butts's thick eyebrows shot up, and a rough bark of a chuckle escaped him. "Salt in your sugar?"

Gertie gave an emphatic nod. "Of course, he denied it, but I knew he did it."

Butts scratched his head. "Now, see, Miz Bogart, I got a problem with people saying they *know* things. Hear it all the time, but usually it's just something they've conjured up in their own minds. Did you see him put salt in your sugar?"

"No." Gertie was getting agitated because Butts didn't seem to believe her. "He went back to the hall where they had the kitchens set up after everybody had gone for the day. A security guard saw him. Julian said he'd come back for his jacket, so the guard didn't follow him into the hall, which he should've done because the contest rules stated that nobody could be in the kitchen area after hours unattended. The next day the stuff in my sugar canister was about half salt."

"That's what we call circumstantial evidence, Miz Bogart. It's not solid evidence like, say"—he scrunched up his eyes as though searching for a case in point—"like a fingerprint. Never get you a conviction in a court of law."

"I didn't need to get a conviction. I *knew* he did it," Gertie insisted, and she had a stubborn set to her jaw. She knew what she knew and she wasn't backing down. "I was beating the pants off him, and he was as mad as a hornet about it. Big-time chef at a fancy San Francisco hotel getting bested by a woman from Missouri who wasn't even a chef. His ego couldn't take it."

"Reckon they had enough egos up there in New York City to go around." He flashed a crooked grin at Gertie. "This cooking contest went on for more than one day?"

"We cooked for three days," Gertie told him. "We made two dishes a day the first two days—appetizers, salads, entrees, and bread. After each round was judged, the points were posted. Julian Walker and I were at the top of the list. It was pretty close, but I was ahead. The third day we prepared a dessert and that counted for twenty-five percent of the total score. I made my To-Die-For Chocolate Dessert, and of course, I never thought to taste the sugar before I measured it."

"Understandable," Butts muttered.

"There were a lot of fancy desserts there that day, but my chocolate dessert would've won, except that it was inedible."

"Too salty, eh?"

"I couldn't believe it at first," Gertie said sadly.

"Did you go to the judges with your suspicions?"

"You bet I did! They called Julian Walker in and he denied everything. Put on quite a show. Called me crazy and carried on about never being so insulted in his life. Since I couldn't prove it, they gave the grand prize to him. I ended up with a thousand dollars, barely enough to pay for my trip. I never wanted to see that man again."

Tess squeezed Gertie's hand, cautioning her to be careful about voicing her opinion of Julian Walker so frankly. Gertie cleared her throat and went on, "I didn't even know he was in Victoria Springs until I walked into the country club last night."

"Must've brought all that stuff in New York back, your arch enemy standing right in front of you like that. Brought it back to him, too. I'm beginning to understand why he ordered you out of his kitchen."

"Chief," Tess inserted, "Julian Walker wasn't Gertie's arch enemy. He was just an unpleasant man who once cheated her out of a cooking prize."

"She thinks," Butts corrected.

"How else could that salt have gotten in my sugar canister?" Gertie demanded. "None of the other contestants was close enough to winning for a stunt like that to put them on top. And none of them had salt in their sugar, either."

"Like I said, Miz Bogart. Circumstantial. But you believe it, so that makes it real for you." Butts squinted at her thoughtfully. "You walk into the man's kitchen and see the guy you believe cheated you out of fifty grand. Got a good job with the country club. Ain't no justice, you think. Quite a shock. Bet you went off like a rocket."

"She did not *go off*," Tess protested. "She went about her business and tried to ignore him."

"But he wouldn't let you ignore him, isn't that right, Miz Bogart?"

"Nobody could ignore the man, the way he strutted around that kitchen." Gertie seemed to catch herself and shot a furtive glance at Tess. "He complained when I didn't leave, is all. I let it go in one ear and out the other. I was there for Tess, and I didn't care what he thought about it. Besides, it wasn't just me. He was yelling at Paula Overton and those two high school boys, too."

Butts wrote in his tablet for several moments. Gertie sent a troubled look toward Tess, who tried not to look anxious and smiled encouragingly. Butts could not actually think Gertie was a murderer, could he?

Finally, Butts flipped the tablet closed and stood to thrust it back into his hip pocket. Planting his hands on his hips, he looked down at Gertie and delivered his bombshell. "By the way, the only identifiable print on the murder weapon was yours, Miz Bogart. Nice clear thumb print up next to the blade."

Tess wanted to smack him. He'd been holding back that bit of information for the most strategic moment.

Gertie went white.

Tess bolted to her feet. "She touched the butcher knife earlier. She was going to use it to cut the shower cake, but Julian gave her a cake knife instead."

"You saw this?"

Tess nodded. Actually, she had heard it, but that was close enough. Now was certainly not the time to volunteer any information about the charges and countercharges Gertie and Julian Walker had exchanged in the pantry when he gave her the cake knife. Gertie didn't mention it, either. It wasn't relevant, Tess told herself.

Butts looked back at Gertie for a moment, then walked toward the entry hall. "Keep yourself available, Miz Bogart," he called just before the door thumped shut behind him.

Gertie got slowly to her feet, wadding her apron in both hands. "I shouldn't have said those things about Julian Walker, but I get so mad every time I think about how he cheated me out of that prize."

"It would upset anyone, Gertie. Don't worry about it."

Tess's words did not ease the worry creases etched in Gertie's face. "Chief Butts wants to arrest me."

"Oh, Gertie, that's not true. Why, he's known you for years."

"We don't know each other very well, hardly enough to speak. And Butts wants to wrap up the murder investigation. You heard him say it yourself. People are going to be after him to solve this murder. I may be the one he decides to pin it on."

"Pin what on?" Nedra Yates, the housekeeper, was standing in the kitchen doorway, her bucket of cleaning supplies in one hand. She was late, and they hadn't heard her come in the back door. "Saw Butts leave. What'd he want?"

"There was a murder at the country club last night," Tess told her. "Gertie and I were there for my shower, so naturally the chief had to question us. It's doesn't mean anything."

"Who?"

Tess looked at her quizzically. She could usually interpret Nedra's conversational snippets, but right now her mind wasn't performing at its peak. "I'm sorry?"

"Who died?" Nedra amended impatiently.

"Julian Walker, the chef."

Nedra shook her head; she'd never heard of him. She lifted her bony shoulders in the faded plaid shirt, which she wore with faded jeans, her usual work uniform. "Strange."

"Yes," Tess agreed.

"Car stalled," Nedra said, having dispensed with conversation about the murder. "Walked to a garage. Gotta work now." Nedra rarely spoke in complete sentences.

"Aren't you going to have breakfast first?" Tess asked.

"Nope. Got a candy bar. At the garage." She trudged through the dining room and paused in the parlor to peer more closely at Gertie. "Look bad peaked," she pronounced like some doom-saying oracle and continued on through the parlor and up the stairs.

Gertie released her wadded apron. "She's going to be a bundle of cheer today. Must be mad about her car quitting on her." She heaved a long breath. "She thinks *she's* got problems."

"She's just Nedra being Nedra," Tess told her. "You know how she is."

Gertie nodded, but made no move to leave the parlor. "I'll fix something for your dinner before I go home."

"Don't do that, Gertie. Dad has already said he's taking all of us, including Luke, out for dinner tonight. You just take care of the breakfasts, and we'll manage the rest."

"Are you sure?"

"Very sure."

"Well, I'll finish cleaning up the kitchen and see that I have everything I need for tomorrow morning. That sweet Curt wants waffles. I made plenty of cookies ahead of time and put them in the freezer. Growing boys are always hungry." Having raised two sons, Gertie was partial to Curt. "I just hope—" Her voice broke and she wiped her eyes with her apron. "Sorry to be so weepy, Tess."

"It'll be all right, Gertie." Tess gave her a hug.

"But Chief Butts acted like he really does think I killed Julian Walker."

"He can't make an arrest on what he thinks. As I told you last night, there are better suspects than you."

Gertie shook her head. "But it's my thumb print he's got on the murder weapon."

"We explained that."

She shook her head. "I don't know, Tess. I got a real bad feeling about this."

"Listen, if Butts actually gets serious about charging you, we'll just have to find the real killer."

As Gertie looked at her with hope in her eyes, Tess could only pray that the situation didn't get that serious.

Chapter 10

Madison stood before a full-length mirror, watching the seamstress pin up the hem of the maid-of-honor gown. She was a vision of youthful feminine loveliness in the yellow silk.

"You're going to steal the show in that dress," Tess said. "Nobody will even see me."

Madison flashed a brilliant smile. "I *do* look good in yellow." Modesty was not one of her virtues, though she had others to make up for it. "How do you think I should wear my hair for the wedding?"

"Down, like it is now, will be perfect," Tess told her. "We could pull it up on the sides and pin a cluster of daisies in it."

"Rad!" She clapped her hands in delight. "Oh, weddings are so romantic."

"Don't move, miss," said the steamstress around the straight pins clamped between her lips. A petite Asian woman, she was called Tandy—not her real name, which was difficult to pronounce.

Madison giggled. "Oops, sorry."

Tess envied all that teenage energy. Even after an overseas flight from Paris, little sleep the night before, and a shopping trip with her mother earlier, Madison bubbled with it. She would undoubtedly crash later in the afternoon.

Tess sank back in her chair and let her heavy eyes drift closed. Within seconds, she was dropping off to sleep. She shook her head and sat up straight. She couldn't let down yet. After they left the seamstress, she had to drop Madison by Dahlia and Maurice's house, where the rest of her family had gone already for a late lunch. If she could get Dahlia alone for a minute, she'd quiz her about the rumors concerning Julian Walker that Dahlia had mentioned at the shower.

From there, she'd go to the country club and talk to Paula Overton about the food for the wedding reception.

"What color is Cinny's dress?" Madison asked.

Cinny was Tess's only bridesmaid. She hadn't wanted a big wedding, but once Dahlia got into it, it had kept getting more and more elaborate. Tess had held the line on attendants, though. Madison and Cinny were all she wanted, except for the friends who would handle the guest book and serve at the reception. Luke had asked his assistant, Sidney Lawson, to be his best man and Curt to serve as groomsman. Two of Luke's friends would be ushers, one of them being Cody Yount, Cinny's as-yet-unofficial fiance.

Dahlia had had to accept the small wedding party, but she had let herself go with the decorations for the church and for the reception at the country club. Since the Forrests were paying for all the flowers, Tess let her have her head, knowing everything would be lovely, if somewhat more showy than she'd intended in the beginning. Fortunately, Luke had no strong feeling on the subject one way or another. He said he just wanted to marry Tess and avoid offending any of her relatives in the process.

Tess had almost drifted to sleep again when Madison said, "Tess! You didn't answer my question."

"Oh, sorry." Tess blinked and smiled at Maddie. "What did you ask me?"

"What color is Cinny's dress?"

"Sort of a soft rust color. In the right light, it has a pink tinge to it. It'll go with the daisies and salmon-colored roses, and it looks great with her blond hair."

Madison surveyed her reflection in the full-length mirror. "I'm going to have a red-and-white wedding."

Tess laughed. "Not for several years yet, I hope."

Madison rolled her dark eyes. "Of course not! I'll graduate from college first."

"I should hope so."

She grinned impishly. "Mother will kill me if I don't."

"Do you have the groom picked out yet?" Tess asked teasingly.

"No," Madison replied in all seriousness. "I'll probably fall madly in love during my junior or senior year in college. I'm sure it won't be any of the boys I go to school with in Paris."

"Got it all planned, have you? But I seem to remember you were pretty infatuated with somebody named Danny last Christmas."

"Danny who?"

How soon they forget, Tess thought. "I don't remember, just Danny. Curt teased you about him unmercifully."

"Curt's a pest." She was thoughtful for a moment. "You must mean the Danny whose father's a career army officer."

"Yes, I remember your mentioning that."

Madison dismissed the subject. "He's a jerk. If you want to know the truth, most of the boys at my school are totally clueless. No class, if you know what I mean. Although . . . there is this new boy, his father got stationed in Paris in April. His name's Kyle. He's already asked me to his senior prom next year."

"That's nice," Tess murmured, unable to stifle a yawn.

"I guess, but that's a whole year from now. I told him I couldn't possibly schedule something that far in advance. I'm keeping my options open."

Trying not to laugh, Tess studied Madison's profile. Her

pretty sister was perfectly serious. Madison was more like
Dahlia than her own mother in personality as well as looks.
From all Tess had heard from her father and her late Aunt
Iris, Dahlia had been the belle of every teenage social func-
tion she ever attended. Tess's father had once said that
Dahlia had had boys hanging around the house vying for
her attention or tying up the family phone line from the day
she turned fourteen until she left for college, where she'd
chosen Maurice Forrest from among her many beaus and
married him the summer following their senior year.

The dressmaker stuck the last pin in the hem of Madison's gown and sat back on her heels. "It's a pleasure making a dress for such a pretty young lady."

"That's kind of you to say," Madison said sincerely.

"You can take it off now," Tandy told her. As Madison
went into the next room to change, Tandy added, "I'll have
the dress ready by tomorrow. I can bring it to Iris House, if
you like."

"That would be a great help, Tandy. Thank you," Tess
said, grateful that she could cross "pick up Madison's
dress" off her to-do list.

An hour later, Tess dropped Madison at the Forrest
house. She managed to get Dahlia alone in the foyer for a
few minutes to quiz her concerning the rumors circulating
about Julian Walker.

"You're as bad as Cinny," Dahlia said. "She's called
twice today, wanting me to give her all the juicy details."
She smiled fondly. "It's making her crazy that I won't."
She studied Tess seriously. "Oh, well, I don't suppose it
matters if I tell you now. One of the women in my bridge
club said she thought Julian's wife was involved with
another man."

"Who?"

"The man, you mean?" Dahlia shook her head. "Rosa
didn't know, or at least that's what she said. It seems her
daughter told her she saw Raylene Walker going into that

shabby little motel on the highway west of town. Though, heaven knows, I can't imagine *that* place as a romantic rendezvous." She pursed her lips. "Still, what other reason would she have for being there?"

Tess supposed Raylene could have gone there for a reason other than to meet a man, but at the moment she couldn't think of one. Raylene was having an affair, which was no more than Tess had already concluded from the conversations she'd overheard between Raylene and the two men. "If you hear anything more, will you tell me, Aunt Dahlia? I'm very worried about Gertie. Finding Julian's body has really unnerved her."

"Of course, dear, I'll tell you anything I learn. I regret that Gertie had the bad luck to discover the body, but I'm sure she will calm down. And I would think you have enough to do for the wedding to keep from getting involved in the investigation."

"I'm sure Chief Butts would agree with you, but he came by Iris House this morning and gave Gertie the third degree. It seems her thumb print was the only identifiable print on the murder weapon."

Dahlia gasped.

Tess went on, "We explained that she'd picked it up earlier in the pantry, but I'm not sure the chief was convinced."

"Our Gertie a murderer? That is utterly preposterous."

"Of course it is," Tess agreed.

Dahlia tapped her patent-leather clad foot, looking worried now. "I'll talk to Rosa again when I have a chance. Maybe she knows more than she told me."

"Thanks, Aunt Dahlia."

As she drove to the country club, Tess forced herself to focus on nailing down the catering service for the reception. She had an appointment to discuss it with Paula Overton in a half-hour.

Chapter 11

"Come on in the office, Tess," Paula said, leading the way briskly to the small, boxy room next to the business suite, which Julian Walker had used as his office. Tess was certain Paula had never been allowed to meet with anyone there when Julian was alive, but then she'd probably had no need to.

Tess noticed that Paula seemed to stand a little straighter and speak with more confidence than when she'd been under Julian's thumb. She wore no hairnet today. Instead, her hair was pulled back and secured with a clasp at the nape of her neck. Now, Paula skirted the small desk to sit in the chair behind it. A crystal vase containing fresh-picked roses sat on one side of the desk. Tess had never seen any flowers in the office when it was Julian's. Behind Paula, the room's only window looked out on the twelfth fairway. Opening a desk drawer, she pulled out a manila folder with *Darcy-Fredrik Reception* scrawled on the tab.

Tess took the only other seat in the room, a steel-framed, armless chair with padded back and seat covered with a nubby, wine-colored fabric. "I know it may be difficult for you to get everything together for the wedding reception in just two weeks, Paula, but I do hope you can do it. I don't know how I'd find another caterer at this late date."

Paula smiled at Tess, tossed back a strand of brown hair that had come loose from the clasp, and opened the folder. Suddenly Tess realized why Paula looked so much livelier today. She wore makeup. Tess didn't recall ever seeing her with blusher and lip gloss before, much less mascara and eyeliner. Perhaps Paula had thought that without makeup she would be less obtrusive, able to fade into the woodwork to escape Julian's notice. On the other hand, Julian had probably disapproved of makeup on the kitchen help. Tess could just hear him: *You're not here to look pretty*.

"It'll be hectic," Paula admitted, "but I can do it, so you can put your mind at rest."

Tess exhaled a long breath and sank back in her chair. "What a relief. I wasn't sure what you'd do now, but it sounds as if you'll be staying in Victoria Springs for a while yet."

"I have eight months left in my apprenticeship," Paula said, as if her staying on were a foregone conclusion.

"But without Julian to supervise . . ."

Paula waved a dismissive hand. "Oh, Mr. Baskin and I have solved that problem. He has asked Bill Humphrey, the chef at the Hilltop Hotel, to supervise my work. We'll have to get the COA committee to approve it, but I'm sure that will be no problem since Bill is a member and a former officer. Bill will come by a couple times a week to meet with me and go over my menus. Otherwise, I'll be the country club chef until my apprenticeship ends—in reality, if not in name. I'm so excited." She was practically preening, clearly very pleased with her new situation. "Mr. Baskin even gave me a raise in salary, and I get to hire an assistant."

"This has all turned out very well for you, then," Tess observed. And that's putting it mildly, she added to herself. In one day, Paula had gone from a frightened and subdued assistant trying to please Julian Walker, an impossible task in itself, with the strong possibility of losing her appren-

ticeship, to the country club chef, with, it appeared, full
discretion in creating menus and hiring kitchen help.

"Better than I had hoped," Paula replied frankly as she
scanned the contents of the folder.

Tess studied her bent head, wondering *when* Paula had
hoped for an improvement in her situation—before
Julian's death or after.

"You might even be able to stay on as chef when your
apprenticeship ends," Tess said.

Paula looked up. "I'm hoping it works out that way. I
know I can do the job. It's just that Julian never let me do
anything except scut work before. It was very frustrating."

"He didn't trust you with more responsibility?"

Paula hesitated, then said, "Frankly, I think he was
afraid I'd show him up if he turned me loose in the kitchen.
He had a very fragile ego and—well, never mind." She
seemed to have realized that speaking ill of the dead to a
club member might not be the politically correct thing to
do. "Even though I'm in charge of the kitchen now, I know
I'm on probation. I want to do an outstanding job with
your reception, Tess, and if you are pleased, I hope you
will put in a good word for me with your uncle."

If Paula was soliciting people to give her a good reference with board members, she had evidently already begun
her campaign to be named the country club chef at the end
of her apprenticeship.

"Fair enough," Tess agreed.

Paula studied her for an instant. "I must sound cold,
talking about my new job and future possibilities. But I
won't pretend I liked Julian or that I'm grieving for him.
I'm sorry he was murdered, but it happened and I want to
make the most of whatever opportunities I have now."

"I understand," Tess said in a noncommittal tone.

Paula hesitated, as though she wanted to say more in her
own defense, then decided against it, perhaps concluding
that would be protesting too much. She pushed the folder
across the desk so that Tess could see the page on top.

"Here's the menu you and Julian came up with. Beef brisket for the entrée; with shrimp cocktail; twice-baked cheese potatoes; green beans almondine; and green, fruit and pasta salads."

"That's right," Tess said.

"Nothing unique here."

"Well—"

"I was wondering," Paula said, "if we might tweak the menu a bit."

"What did you have in mind?"

"We could add another entrée—chicken or perhaps fish. People nowadays are so fat-conscious, some of them prefer not to eat beef. And in case there are any vegetarians in attendance, I'll do a small meatless main dish, too. You being a Darcy and all, this will be an important social event, the first big gala I'll be in charge of, so we want to do it up properly for both our benefits."

"I think you're exaggerating its importance," Tess said.

"Oh, no. You must know how influential your aunt and uncle are in this town."

"I suppose," Tess agreed, and of course, she did know. "Anyway, I like the idea of more choices."

"Great! I have an excellent recipe for stuffed chicken breasts and another for glazed salmon steaks. I'll have to think about the meatless entrée. Hmm, let me go through my recipes. I'll come up with something you'll like."

"I have the utmost confidence in you," Tess assured her, "so I'll leave it in your hands."

Paula made a note on the menu. "Now, about the green beans almondine." She wrinkled her nose. "That's so—well, ordinary, don't you think?"

Tess shrugged. "It's an old standby. Most people like it."

"What if we substitute a vegetable medley? That would be a little different, and so much more colorful."

Tess was not married to the idea of green beans almondine. At the time she and Julian Walker had met, she'd been searching frantically for a dressmaker and had gone along with the menu Julian suggested. But Paula seemed to enjoy adding her special touches to the menu, which probably meant she would take more pride in preparing and presenting the buffet if she were allowed some leeway. "All right."

"And, of course, we'll have champagne—and fruit punch for those who don't drink alcohol."

Tess nodded.

"Who is doing your wedding cake?" Paula asked.

"The woman who makes most of the wedding cakes in Victoria Springs, Janet Dahl. Her cakes are wonderful."

Paula frowned a little. Had she hoped to prepare the cake herself? Probably, as it would provide a perfect opportunity to show off her cake-decorating skills.

"Is she making the groom's cake, as well?"

"Yes."

"Too bad," Paula murmured with a sigh. "I made top grades in decorated cakes at the institute."

Julian had not offered to make the cakes, which had been fine with Tess, as she'd often admired Janet's cakes; and she had no intention of canceling her order with Janet two weeks prior to the wedding. "I'm sure you'll have a chance to use those skills at another time."

Paula nodded. "You're right." She perused the menu again. "Now, about the ice sculpture for the centerpiece."

"That was Aunt Dahlia's idea. Julian said he'd take care of it. Do you know somebody who could do it?"

"You're looking at her. We made them at the institute. I never sculpted a bride and groom but I can do a large swan. Surrounded by flowers, it's quite showy."

"A swan sounds wonderful, but that's a lot of work for you with the food preparation."

"I'm not afraid of work, Tess."

"Do it then."

Paula smiled happily. It was another opportunity to show off, Tess mused, and then wondered why she was having these critical thoughts about Paula. But then she knew why.

Julian's death had put Paula in a position to become the next country club chef. Otherwise, it might have taken her several years to capture such a prize position.

"I guess that about does it, unless there's something else you'd like to add to the menu."

"It sounds perfect as it is," Tess told her.

Paula closed the folder and returned it to the desk drawer. Since Tess had her alone she took the opportunity to ask a few questions.

"Have the police been back here today?"

"Bright and early," Paula said, leaning back in her chair. "Crime scene technicians went over the pantry and kitchen like hounds sniffing for a rabbit. Thank goodness I had no breakfast to prepare this morning. It took two hours to clean up after them. What a mess, powder everywhere and nothing put back in its place."

Tess could sympathize, as she had personally witnessed the disarray left in the wake of a police search when Chief Butts and his deputies had ransacked Iris House, including Tess's apartment, while investigating the murder of one of Tess's guests earlier that year.

"Was Chief Butts here?"

Paula's eyes clouded. "Yes. He questioned Mr. Baskin, the office help, the golf pro. And me, of course." Her brow furrowed. "He has the idea that Julian was about to fire me. I told him there was no way Julian would have done that because he needed somebody to do the dirty work around here. But Chief Butts said I might have to go down to the station for more questions."

"Julian did threaten to let you go."

Her lips thinned. "He wouldn't have done it," she said shortly, a refrain she'd been repeating stubbornly since the discovery of the chef's body.

"Perhaps not, but if he had, what would you have done?"

"There would've been options. I would have phoned the institute and asked them to give me another apprenticeship. Actually, I might have been better off."

"Before Julian was killed, but now . . ." Tess remembered Paula saying last night that it wouldn't be easy to find another apprenticeship, and that Julian would probably blackball her.

"You sound like Chief Butts. He actually told me I was a suspect. I can't believe anybody would think I could have killed Julian, no matter how cranky he was."

Interesting choice of word, "cranky," Tess thought. Julian had been much more than cranky in his dealing with Paula. He'd been mean and overbearing and threatening. Tess could not imagine how Paula had tolerated such treatment for four months while looking forward to eight more months of it—if she was lucky enough not to be fired. Tess could imagine how Paula might have reached the end of her tolerance and decided to do something to change the situation.

"I'm sure you aren't the only suspect on the chief's list."

"I certainly hope not! I am not a violent person, Tess."

"Somebody who was here last night was."

She chewed her bottom lip for a moment. "I know. I may have made a mistake . . ." She paused and looked down at her hands.

"What do you mean?"

Paula looked up. "I wondered, after what happened— well, maybe I shouldn't have hired Craig Young and his friend."

How had they gone from Chief Butts's suspect list to the two high school boys? "How *did* that happen?" Tess asked.

"I'm renting the garage apartment behind Craig's parents' house. When Julian asked me to find a couple of people to help with the barbecue, I naturally thought of Craig. He seemed glad of the job and suggested Jeff, one of his friends, as the second helper."

"But now you regret hiring them. Why?"

"Oh, they did the job OK. It's just . . ." She paused as though to choose her next words carefully. "Craig has a terrible temper. He's been in trouble at school several times for fighting. Once he sent another boy to the hospital. His parents were terrified the other parents would sue, but I guess they didn't. I haven't heard any more about it."

"Julian was pretty rough on the boys," Tess mused.

"And it was totally uncalled for. They couldn't help being a little late, and once they got here, they did what they were told."

"Do you really think Craig could have stabbed Julian?"

"I wouldn't have, except . . ."

"What?"

"I probably shouldn't say anything."

But it was obvious she was dying to. "If you know anything, Paula, you have a duty to turn it over to the police."

"It's just—well, I did mention it to Chief Butts. After Julian came out on the patio and called Craig and Jeff lazy no-goods in front of the guests, I heard Craig tell Jeff that nobody talked to him like that and got away with it. He was so angry he was actually trembling."

"Julian did seem to have that effect on a lot of people." But would any of them kill him for it? Would Craig Young?

"The police will question both boys," Tess went on.

Paula nodded, looking faintly alarmed. "Chief Butts promised me he wouldn't reveal to Craig who told him about the threat."

Tess didn't think it would be difficult for Craig to figure it out, though. "Is there anybody else at the club that Julian had ongoing problems with?"

"He and the golf pro had words a few times. Julian didn't want Johnny to give Raylene free golf lessons, but Johnny did, anyway. After that, it was obvious Julian had no use for Johnny."

"How did Johnny feel about him?"

"I think he just mostly ignored Julian. When Julian told Johnny he didn't want his wife coming to the barbecue last night, Johnny told him he was telling the wrong person, that he had no control over Julian's wife. I saw her last night, even though she had to know Julian didn't want her here. And then I saw Julian and Johnny talking."

"About Raylene's presence at the barbecue?"

"I don't know what it was about, but it didn't look like a friendly chat."

"When did this talk take place?"

"Maybe an hour before Julian's body was found. They were standing just inside the reception area, near the patio doors, when I made one of my trips from the kitchen to the patio."

"Paula, this could be important. Did you hear what they were saying?"

"The only thing I heard was Julian telling Johnny to make some excuse to stop Raylene's golf lessons. And then Johnny said something like he'd be glad to if Julian would stay away from his wife." She smiled ironically. "Frankly, I'd never seen Julian say a word to Wendy."

"Johnny told Julian to stay away from Wendy?"

Paula nodded.

"Why would he have thought Julian might have anything to do with his wife?" Was it possible Julian Walker had been having an extramarital affair, too?

"No idea."

Nor had Tess, but it might be interesting to find out. "Anybody else who's had problems with Julian?"

"Not that I can testify to, but I'm in the kitchen most of the time. I wouldn't have known if he argued with other people in the office or other places around the club."

Evidently she wasn't going to reveal anything else that was useful. And Tess suspected, if she could, Paula would be eager to provide other suspects to take some of the heat off herself.

"Has Mrs. Walker been here since it happened?"

"No. I called her this morning to tell her she could pick up Julian's things from the office any time. She said I should leave Julian's belongings alone, that she'd come by when she could. She was sort of huffy with me. I probably should have waited a day or two to call her." She glanced around the small office. "I need to use the desk now, so I put Julian's things in a box." She indicated a pasteboard carton in a corner.

"Where is the Walker house?"

"In that new addition south of here. Dunningworth Green, I think it's called."

"Would you like me to take the box to Raylene? I have to go right by that addition on my way home."

"Oh, that would be good—if you don't mind." Paula wrote the address on a scrap of paper and handed it to Tess. Then she jumped up. "As you can see, there's not much room in here. I keep stumbling over that box." She skirted the desk to pick up the carton and give it to Tess.

They said their good-byes and Tess left, congratulating herself on coming up with a valid excuse to call on Raylene Walker. When she had reached her car and set the box in the passenger-side front seat, she glanced around to see if anyone was watching her. Nobody was about except a greenskeeper who was too far away to notice Tess, and Paula's office with its single window wasn't on that side of the club.

Satisfied she was not being observed, Tess went through the box, lifting out pens, a calculator, magazines, two framed certificates, and several folders containing notes and menus for previous events that Julian must have been in charge of.

The last thing in the box was a desk diary. Tess leafed through it and read the cryptic notes, all of which seemed to have to do with business. There were several names with phone numbers beside them. Tess recognized most of the names as members of the country club. Nothing there that might be a clue to Julian's murderer.

After returning the diary to the box and closing the flaps, she drove away from the country club, turning left instead of right as she exited the grounds. Dunningworth Green, the addition where Raylene Walker lived, wasn't really on her way home—in fact, it was in the opposite direction. But it had been too convenient an opportunity to talk to Raylene Walker to pass up.

Chapter 12

Raylene Walker stood, concealed behind her living room drapes. With one hand, she opened a slit where the two sides of the drapes met, and watched Chief Desmond Butts drive away in his patrol car. Her heart was thumping at twice its normal rate. It couldn't be good, letting herself get so agitated, in her condition. She took several deep breaths, trying to slow her heart rate and make herself think of something besides the conversation she'd just had with Butts. But it was impossible to dismiss the situation in which she was embroiled. She'd thought yesterday that things couldn't get any worse. How wrong she had been!

She had often wondered how her life might have turned out if she'd refused Julian's marriage proposal and stayed in San Francisco. Until a few months ago, her fantasy had been that instead of marrying Julian, she would have met a young, handsome man. He would have already been established in a well-paying profession—a doctor or a lawyer, say—and he would have fallen hopelessly in love with her. They would take long walks and have endless conversations because, of course, she would be able to talk to him about anything. They would have married, moved to the suburbs, and had a couple of beautiful children—a boy first, and then a girl.

Sometimes, she added her mother to the fantasy. In one version, her mother had come to her senses when Raylene left home, admitted she had a problem with alcohol, and joined AA. In another version, her mother had never been an alcoholic at all. Either way, her mother was sober and visited Raylene often, where she was thrilled with her daughter's beautiful house; her lovely, well-behaved children; and her handsome, devoted husband. She was, of course, a doting grandmother who often stayed with the children while Raylene and Gregory (that was the fantasy husband's name) jetted off for a holiday in some romantic hideaway in France or Italy.

Raylene's father never figured into her fantasies because by then she had begun to suspect that no man, with the single and amazing exception of Gregory, could be trusted. Recently, she'd begun to hope that she'd found her Gregory, but he'd proved himself unworthy of her trust.

Certainly she did not trust Chief Desmond Butts, with his good-old-country-boy act. When he'd first arrived at her door, he'd apologized for intruding on her at such a trying time, but he needed to clear up a few loose threads in his investigation. He asked her about the members of the country club and the people who had worked there with Julian. Had any of them been a special friend of Julian's? Had she and Julian socialized with them? Had Julian had trouble with a member or another employee—or anybody else, for that matter?

He had led her to believe that the investigation was at a dead end already and he was grasping at straws. She had begun to relax, and then he said, in the same matter-of-fact voice as before, "It's come to my attention, Miz Walker, that you have been having an extramarital affair. I will need that man's name, of course, because I will have to talk to him. I assure you, I will handle it in private."

At which point, Raylene had felt as if she'd fallen off a tall building and had the breath knocked out of her. Her mouth had dropped open, and for a moment, she'd been unable to speak. Finally, she'd rallied and said, "I—I don't know who told you such a vicious piece of trash, but it's not true. I loved my husband."

"Well, small towns are hotbeds of gossip, as I'm sure you must know by now. I'm certain you will want to stop these lies."

"I don't know how I can do that," she ventured suspiciously. "People want to believe the worst of other people."

"Perhaps you and this other man were just friends. If I could talk to him, I'm sure he'd clear everything up."

"There is no other man! Surely you aren't suggesting, in the midst of grieving for my dead husband and trying to get his body released so I can give him a decent burial, that I give you the name of every man I know so you can harass them."

"If you want to stop the talk—"

Raylene had lost it then. "I don't give a shit about the talk! I have far more serious things to worry about—like what I am going to do now that my husband is gone."

Butts had studied her with those bushy eyebrows lifted, as if she'd suddenly metamorphosed into a strange new life form. "You think about it," he'd said mildly. "I'll be in touch." She didn't think she had imagined the hint of menace in that last remark.

She had trailed him to the door, not bothering to respond to his "Good day," before she closed and bolted it behind him. Good day? Her "good day" had started when she'd phoned the insurance company to ask when she could expect the life insurance check. She'd told them the medical examiner hadn't released Julian's body yet, but she was sure to have the death certificate any day.

The woman had said she shouldn't expect the check right away. They'd been in touch with the medical examiner and discovered Julian was murdered. We can't issue a check, she'd said, until we're sure you—rather, I mean, until we know who killed your husband.

I don't understand why you have to know anything beyond the cause of death, Raylene had objected. It's company policy, the woman had said. Of course, what she'd meant was that if Raylene was convicted of killing her husband—which they were no doubt hoping would be the case—she could kiss that quarter-million good-bye.

It was one thing to be reminded that you were probably a suspect in your husband's murder by some strange woman in the insurance company office in Connecticut. It was quite another to have the chief of police suggest you have a lover that your husband knew about, which might give you or the lover—or both—a motive for murder and that if you were going to claim otherwise, you might be required to prove it.

Watching Chief Butts depart her house, she realized that if Butts knew about the affair, others might as well. She decided then and there that she would have Julian's body cremated and would scatter the ashes to the four winds. She wouldn't subject herself to a funeral service, even a small, private memorial service, where everybody in attendance might think she'd had reason to kill her husband. Fortunately, Julian had cut himself off from whatever family he had years ago, so she wouldn't know how to notify them of his death if she'd wanted to.

Meantime, she had to go to the bank and have Julian's name taken off their joint accounts. There was enough money in the combined checking and savings accounts to see her through three or four months if she budgeted carefully. Well, she certainly knew how to do that. Before her marriage, she'd always been in a financial bind. The mortgage policy they'd taken out would leave her with the house free and clear. Of course, the company probably wouldn't release that money, either, until the investigation was closed. She had meant to call them today, but after talking to the woman in Connecticut yesterday, she decided to wait.

It would surely be a waste of time to call either company again until the investigation was closed, assuming Desmond Butts would look beyond her for a suspect. Besides, it wouldn't do to appear too greedy, too eager to get her hands on the money. Maybe she would even go to church Sunday, despite the fact that she hadn't darkened the door of a church for years. It would look as if she were seeking solace from her grief.

She wished she had somewhere to go right now, any-where to get out of the house for a while. She'd lived in Victoria Springs for a year without making any real friends, except for Wendy Linzy, who was the last person on earth she could go to now. A couple of her neighbors had made overtures, and one had invited her and Julian to a backyard cookout. Julian had been absolutely beastly about it. Why would he want to spend an evening drinking beer and listening to some redneck's stupid jokes while the couple's two kids ran wild? If she wanted to go, she could go alone. Of course, she hadn't gone. She hadn't known how she would explain Julian's absence. Instead, she had called the neighbor and said she wasn't feeling well. The next day when the neighbor had stopped Julian in the yard to ask how Raylene was feeling, he'd been so rude to the woman that she'd never come to call on Ray-lene again. Maybe now, Raylene thought with a sigh, she could make new friends. It was pathetic that she could not think of a single person whom she might ask to come and keep her company for a while.

For one instant, she started to the phone to call *him*, but then she remembered that he wanted nothing more to do with her. Contact would be unwise, in any case. Nor was she going to put herself into position to be rejected again.

She took an angry swipe at sudden tears. Damn all men. She was never going to be dependent on one again.

She wandered into the kitchen, poured a cup of decaf-feinated coffee left from breakfast, and put it in the microwave to heat. As she was removing the cup from the microwave, the sound of the door chimes made her start, and she spilled hot coffee on her skirt. Muttering a curse, she set the cup down, grabbed a dish towel and wiped the stain, then went to the front window to peek between the drapes and see who was there.

Tess Darcy stood on her front porch, holding a cardboard box in her arms. Oh, God, not now. What was *she* doing here? Before last night, Raylene had liked Tess, who had treated her with kindness whenever they ran into each other at the country club. She had even insisted that Raylene call her by her first name.

But now, Raylene thought she knew how people being stalked must feel—trapped and desperate. Last evening, Tess Darcy had been everywhere she turned, listening in on Raylene's private conversations. It dawned on Raylene then that Butts's information about the affair could have come from Tess. She tried to remember exactly what had been said in those conversations, but she had apparently blocked out the most painful parts.

Now, like some clinging specter that would not go away, here was that red-haired busybody on her doorstep.

Her first impulse was to not answer the door. Then she remembered that her car was in the driveway, so Tess would know Raylene was avoiding her. Should she risk alienating her?

It occurred to Raylene that if Tess believed she was innocent of Julian's murder, it might help her situation. Tess's family was important in Victoria Springs, and Raylene could certainly use somebody in her corner right now.

Tess might just be paying a sympathy call on a new widow. She struck Raylene as the sort of woman who would do that. Raylene decided she would be polite and get rid of the woman as quickly as possible.

Chapter 13

"Sorry to disturb you," Tess said as soon as Raylene opened the door, "but I was at the country club earlier and Paula asked me to drop off Julian's things."

Raylene's facial muscles tightened, giving her a slightly mummified look. Clearly, she was not over-joyed to see Tess. Or perhaps it was the wrong time to have mentioned Paula. "I *told* her I'd pick them up."

"The box was in the way—well, you know how small that office is. And, since I was coming in this direction anyway, I didn't mind bringing it by."

"I seriously doubt it was in the way." Raylene sniffed. "Paula just couldn't wait a day or two to get rid of every reminder of my husband." She opened the door a little wider, giving Tess just enough room to step inside. If it was an invitation, it was a feeble one, but Tess took advantage of it anyway, and carried the box into the foyer.

Still looking disgruntled, Raylene gazed at Tess for a moment, then turned away, saying, "You'd think Paula would have enough problems, trying to find another apprenticeship, without worrying about a few insignificant little items of Julian's."

Tess followed her into the living room and set the

box on the coffee table. "Actually, she's staying on at the club."

"But she can't finish her apprenticeship without the supervision of a certified chef," Raylene said over her shoulder.

"The chef at the Hilltop Hotel is going to oversee the remainder of her apprenticeship. So she'll be using Julian's office."

Raylene faced her, eyebrows drawing together. "Well, that was fast work. No flies on Paula Overton."

"She does seem to have landed on her feet. She's taking over the chef's duties, for now at least. With a raise in pay, she told me, and she'll be able to hire an assistant."

Raylene gave a disdainful snort. "I'll be surprised if she lasts a month. Julian was always talking about how incompetent she was. He never trusted her enough to give her any responsibilities."

"I got the impression it was more of a personality conflict than incompetence on Paula's part."

Raylene made no attempt to hide her contempt for Paula. "That, too. I know Julian wasn't easy to get along with but Paula's too sensitive, if you ask me."

"Do you think he would have sent her packing before the end of her apprenticeship?"

Raylene gave an emphatic nod. "There's no way she would have lasted the full year. Frankly, I'm surprised Julian hadn't shown her the door already."

"Paula doesn't believe he actually intended to let her go."

"People lie," Raylene stated, as if it was naïve to expect anything else.

Tess glanced around the cream-and-beige living room. It was furnished with a matching burgundy sofa and love seat along with two matching side chairs upholstered in a floral fabric—like a furniture showroom, she thought. "Will you be going back to San Francisco now?"

Restlessly, Raylene straightened a china shepherdess

figurine on the coffee table. She seemed irritated by Tess's question. "There's nothing back there for me. This is my home now."

"Will your family be coming here for the funeral?"

"I have no family—none I'd claim, anyway. Neither did Julian," Raylene said shortly. She remained standing beside the love seat, laying her arm along the back. "I know you're busy with your wedding coming up and all. I won't keep you, Tess." Not the most subtle dismissal Tess had ever heard, but she ignored it.

"There's something I need to discuss with you before I go," she said. As it didn't appear Raylene was going to invite her to make herself comfortable, Tess moved to one of the side chairs and sat down.

Raylene fingered a button at the neck of her dress. From her drawn expression, she seemed to be prickling with resentment, evidently because Tess hadn't taken the hint and left. "I'm not very good company, Tess. I've got a lot on my mind." In spite of wanting Tess gone, she seemed to be straining to be polite.

"This will only take a minute."

Eyeing Tess warily, she walked stiffly around the love seat to perch on the edge of a cushion. In spite of the room's air-conditioned coolness, a drop of sweat trickled from her temple, and she wiped it away with the back of her hand. "What is it?" she said quickly. "I'm sure you understand I have things to do."

"Of course." Tess decided that blunt honesty was the only chance she had of getting Raylene to tell her anything. "I know you and Julian argued last night."

"I don't want to discuss that with you! Don't you think I'm feeling guilty enough because the last words I had with my husband were hateful ones?"

"My point is you and Julian argued over your seeing another man."

"My God," Raylene snorted. "The whole town must be

buzzing with that lie. Chief Butts was just here, blabbing about the same thing."

"Cinny and I overheard your conversation with Julian last night, and I heard you talking to another man earlier in the evening. I had the distinct impression that the first man wanted to end your affair, which was very upsetting for you."

Raylene opened her mouth to speak, but Tess plowed ahead. "I think Julian knew about the affair and, after your conversation with the other man, you decided to smooth things over with your husband. But he wasn't interested."

Mouth still gaping, she stared at Tess. "Did anyone ever tell you you should write fiction?" she said finally.

"I heard you, Raylene."

"My, my, you were certainly busy last night," she said bitterly, "what with your bridal shower and running around listening to people's private conversations. And, of course, you had to report what you *think* you heard to Chief Butts."

There was no point in denying it. "I can't withhold information from the police, even though it might have no bearing on Julian's case."

"Don't you people in this town have anything better to do than to nose around in other people's personal business?"

"Raylene," Tess said gently, "yours and Julian's personal business has become part of a murder investigation."

Raylene paled. "I can't see how."

Tess did not believe she was that obtuse. "The police want to know everything Julian did last night, who he talked to, where he was at any given time."

Raylene wrapped her arms around her stomach, as if to protect herself. "I was on the patio most of the time."

"Except when you were talking to Julian and the other man."

Her mouth twisted. "Married people argue all the time, but Chief Butts seems to be hung up on that disagreement between Julian and me."

"He's checking out a lot of people, not just you. He told me himself he has several people on his suspect list."

"*Suspect*?" Her arms tightened on her stomach and suddenly the blood left her face. Before Tess knew what was happening, Raylene jumped up and ran from the room. Then she heard retching.

Tess followed the sound down the hallway to a bathroom. The door was open and Raylene was hunched over the toilet bowl, braced by both hands planted on either side of the rim.

Tess grabbed a washcloth from a rack and wet it at the sink. She pressed it against Raylene's brow, smoothing her hair back off her forehead. The retching stopped, and Raylene grabbed the wet cloth and staggered upright.

All at once, the confrontations Tess had heard Raylene have with the two men last night and her extreme agitation made much more sense. "Are you pregnant, Raylene?"

Raylene held the washcloth over her face for an instant before she removed it and met Tess's gaze with a nod. "I'm just starting to get morning sickness, except I seem to have it at any time of the day." She wiped her face again and dropped the cloth into the sink. She had retched so violently that tiny red blood vessels streaked the whites of her eyes. She slumped against the sink. "Can't you see I don't feel like making conversation? Just go away and leave me alone."

"You need to lie down," Tess said. "Let me help you to your bedroom."

"No, the couch will do." Spent from the bout of vomiting, she let Tess take her arm and lead her back to the living room, where she lay down on the couch with a deep sigh. "God, I hope this doesn't go on much longer."

"I hear it passes after the first few months."

"Wonderful," Raylene muttered and closed her eyes.

"I don't like to leave you when you're feeling ill," Tess said. "Isn't there someone I could call to come stay with you?"

Raylene struggled to lift her head from the couch. "No! I *am* alone now, so I'd better get used to it. Besides, I don't know why you care about me or how I feel. It's not as if we've ever been close, and frankly, it's none of your business."

"I know it isn't, or it wouldn't be, except that I'm trying to help Chief Butts clarify a few things." No need for Raylene to know that this would be news to Butts. "For one, why Julian was angry enough last night to ask you to leave this house."

She was suspicious. "Why would Chief Butts ask for your help?"

"I know the country club staff and the club members, who's related to whom, and things like that. Raylene, it might be better to tell me why Julian asked you to leave, rather than let Chief Butts conjure up his own reasons."

"Oh, he probably would have changed his mind. He was too upset to be coherent. He didn't want to be a father at his age."

"Are you saying Julian threatened to divorce you because you got pregnant?"

She seemed to have reached the end of her patience with Tess. "I don't have to justify anything to you!" she snarled. "But, yes, that was his initial reaction. He wanted me to get rid of it—damn him. I refused. I want this baby." She closed her eyes and mumbled something under her breath. Then, "God knows I shouldn't have been shocked by Julian's reaction. Every man I've ever known, starting with my father, has betrayed me. Believe me, this child will never know how his father reacted to the news."

"I see. So Julian wanted you to get rid of the baby or move out of the house."

"Neither of which I had any intention of doing!"

Then what had that argument with the other man been about? Tess wondered. In light of the fact that Raylene was pregnant, it now seemed possible that Julian had called his wife a liar because he suspected another man of being the father—somebody who was at the club last night. When Julian left Raylene after the argument, had he gone in search of the other man?

"Your husband may not have wanted a child, but his reaction seems extreme."

Raylene considered her dubiously from her prone position on the couch. "As I said, he was upset. Julian was apt to say anything when he lost his temper. I can't believe I never saw that side of him until after we were married."

"When he left you, he went outside. Is it possible, Raylene, that he went to confront the man you talked with earlier? Isn't it possible Julian didn't believe he was the baby's father?"

Raylene's pinched face radiated the misery of a woman abandoned by the two men in her life. "He was looking for somebody to blame. I'm sure he wanted to believe I'd been unfaithful. That would have relieved him of any responsibility. I suppose he could have fixated on somebody, he might even have wanted to confront him, but he didn't, or at least not in anyone else's hearing, or Chief Butts would have thrown that in my face, too."

"Or Julian could have talked to Jed Baskin about it," Tess commented. "I heard him say he might speak to his boss."

Raylene sat up slowly. "Yes, he did say that."

"Even if he didn't talk to Jed, Raylene, these things have a way of getting out, one way or another."

She got to her feet and straightened her dress. She shook her head. "Julian was so proud, he wouldn't have . . . he couldn't . . ." A tremor of alarm had come into her voice. "I'm sorry, Tess, but you must excuse me now. I have to get out of the house before I go stir-crazy."

"Should you be driving when you're not feeling well?"

"I think I can be the judge of that. I've been taking care of myself since I was seventeen." Giving Tess no chance to linger, she went to the door and opened it.

She ushered Tess out hastily, shut the door, and leaned

back against it. "I tried to be polite, Tess Darcy," she muttered to herself, "but you practically accused me of killing Julian."

Tess found herself on Raylene Walker's doorstep, facing a closed door, having gleaned no concrete evidence to implicate Raylene or anybody else in Julian's murder. Defeated, she walked back to her car.

People lie, Raylene had said.

Well, she was right about that. Tess was sure that Raylene herself had been lying just now. Exactly how much of what she'd said was untrue, Tess didn't know. But she had heard nothing in the conversation between Julian and Raylene to suggest that Julian's fury had resulted simply from being told he was going to be a father. It was entirely possible that the father of Raylene's unborn child was still very much alive and was either employed at the country club or was a member there. And Julian had left the building last night to confront the man. Whoever he was, he'd had a very good reason to shut Julian up for good.

All mere circumstantial evidence, Butts would say, if that. More likely, he'd label it pure speculation.

She'd been in such a hurry to talk to Raylene Walker that she hadn't spoken to Jed Baskin while she was at the country club. The possibility remained that Julian had carried out his threat to lodge a complaint with Jed before he was killed. If so, Jed might know the name of Raylene Walker's lover. But would he tell Tess? Only if he didn't realize he was doing it.

Tess consulted her wristwatch. She should have just enough time to talk to Jed before returning to Iris House to get ready for dinner with her family. Backing out of the Walkers' driveway, she headed toward the country club again.

Chapter 14

A young woman with frizzy blond hair sat at the reception desk leafing through a magazine. Tess had never seen her before, but her name badge read "Kaylynn Vickery."

"Hello," Tess said.

She looked up, pale blue eyes wide. "Oh, hi."

"Is Mr. Baskin in?"

"Yes, but he doesn't want to be disturbed." She tugged on a coil of hair in front of her ear. She seemed tense. Jed had probably reprimanded her for leaving early the evening before and she was afraid of making another mistake. But somebody should tell her she needed to come up with a more discreet response than that.

"Why don't you tell him Tess Darcy is here?"

She frowned. "You're a club member, right?"

"Yes."

"I've been trying to memorize the membership list, and I thought I'd seen your name." Her gaze darted anxiously to the closed door of Jed's office. "If I interrupt him, he'll be mad." Jed must've put the fear of God in her. The poor girl seemed afraid of her own shadow.

"I'll tell you what," Tess said. "I have another piece

of business to take care of. Why don't I check back with you in a little while?"

The tension eased out of her face. "That would be just fine, Miss Darcy."

Tess left the office wondering where Jed Baskin had found Kaylynn. Her lack of poise seemed to make her an unlikely candidate to handle the club's reception area and serve as Jed's secretary. The woman who had held the job before, and who'd left because her husband was transferred out of town, could have tamed a pride of lions with one hand while answering the phone with the other, all without breaking a sweat.

Tess walked down the hall to the kitchen and dining area. She paused at the green room, which was unoccupied, its door standing open. She went in, not looking for anything in particular, but convinced that among the people who'd been in the green room last night, one of them had been the murderer.

When Julian was killed, Gertie and Dahlia had been going in and out of the kitchen, which lay on the other side of the pantry. The murderer had to have entered the pantry from this room.

When Tess pushed the swinging door into the pantry half-open, she could hear somebody humming and moving around in the kitchen on the other side of the second swinging door. That would be Paula Overton happily readying the kitchen kingdom for its new monarch.

Whoever had killed Julian must have been very quiet about it. Noises from the pantry could be heard through the door leading into the kitchen. But then Gertie and Dahlia would have been talking, running water, perhaps clanging pots, and, with Cinny, transporting things from the large dining room. The murder *could* have occurred while they were all out of the kitchen. Still, the risk of being overheard would have been huge. Nobody would intentionally take a risk like that.

The killer must have acted on impulse. Killing the chef in the pantry while three women were wandering around in the area could not have been planned.

The pantry shelves were neatly lined with groceries, and the tile floor shone from a recent waxing. Obviously the crime scene crew had finished there and given Paula the go-ahead to clean up. When Tess let the pantry door swing shut again, she could no longer hear anything from the kitchen. Closing both pantry doors created a barrier that screened out all but the loudest noises.

She walked idly around the green room, skirting a few tables that had been spread with fresh linen cloths. Paula must be getting ready for a luncheon or a small dinner party. Sunlight streaming in between vertical blinds threw narrow stripes across the green carpet.

Tess went to a window, trying to remember if the blinds had been open or closed last night. The room would have been lighted, and if the blinds were open, anybody outside would have had a good view of the interior. She'd passed the green room door several times last night. As she recalled, the door had been closed most of the time. With her mind on other things, she probably wouldn't have noticed if the blinds were open, even if the door had been ajar. Probably at night, they'd been closed.

At some point during the evening, the green room had been used for an impromptu meeting by Jed Baskin, Johnny Linzy, and Wayne Trammell. Dahlia had speculated they'd been discussing the new golf course, so there could well have been other board members in attendance, too. Both the kitchen and the green room were being used—more evidence that the murder was a spur-of-the-moment response. To what? Julian had certainly been in a black mood all evening, but what could he have said or done that made somebody react so violently?

A car drove up outside. Tess parted two of the blinds for a better view. Raylene Walker got out of the car and walked toward the building. Tess suspected she wanted to talk to Jed Baskin, for the same reason that Tess did—to find out what, if anything, Julian had said to Jed after his argument with his wife. Tess doubted that Raylene would have any better luck getting to Jed than she had.

As she removed her fingers to let the blinds fall back into place, she noticed a dark spot on one of the slats. It was the color of old rust, like dried blood. She found the long rod that controlled the blinds and closed them. The spot was barely visible now. She twisted the rod again, opening the blinds, letting slatted sunlight stream in again, and the spot came back into full view.

If it was Julian's blood, the murderer could have touched the blind after killing Julian. More likely, Julian had been stabbed in the green room and later moved into the pantry. But if so, there should have been more blood in the room, and there was no sign that the carpet had been scrubbed or the walls painted since last night. Maybe it wasn't blood, after all—or not Julian's blood. Still, she'd tell Chief Butts about the spot, which the crime scene techs could easily have overlooked.

She went back into the hall and walked to the kitchen door. Paula was stirring something in a large mixing bowl at the work island. Tess rapped on the door frame. Paula looked up and smiled. "Oh, hi, Tess. Do we need to talk about the reception again?"

"No, I'm here to see Jed. I was just wondering. Did the crime scene technicians go over the green room?"

She nodded. "There was dark powder on the outside of the pantry door on that side and also on the one leading out to the hallway, as well as on the carpet around both doors. I cleaned it up this morning."

The two logical places to dust for fingerprints, Tess thought. And clearly there had been no blood on the carpet or walls.

Paula cocked her head, looking questioningly at Tess. "Just wondering," Tess said hastily and hurried away before Paula could quiz her.

She returned to the reception area. Kaylynn was still sitting at her desk, looking at a magazine.

"Is Jed free now?"

Kaylynn shook her head. "I'm awfully sorry."

"Is Raylene Walker in there with him?"

Kaylynn looked bewildered. "No, I haven't seen Mrs. Walker today. Mr. Baskin is still meeting with the board members."

"Oh. Well, I can't wait any longer. Tell Jed I was here and I'll talk to him later."

Tess returned to the hallway. Now where had Raylene gone if not to the manager's office? Could she have wanted something from Julian's office, something that Paula hadn't put in the box Tess had taken to the Walker house? Tess opened the door to the chef's office and peeked in. Nobody there.

Her curiosity rising, she walked far enough down the hallway to see into the kitchen, where Paula Overton was working alone. Frowning, Tess stepped out of sight before Paula saw her.

Raylene was nowhere to be seen. And Tess didn't have time to search for her any longer. She had to go back to Iris House and get ready for dinner out with her family.

Perhaps Raylene had left the club while Tess was looking for her. But when she returned to the parking lot, she saw that Raylene's car was still there. Here was one mystery that would have to remain unsolved, Tess decided, as she reluctantly got into her car.

The interior of the car was sweltering. She started the engine and turned the air-conditioner on full blast. Taking her cell phone from the glove compartment, she dialed the police station, identified herself, and asked to speak to Chief Butts.

"Yeah?" Butts greeted her rudely.

"This is Tess Darcy, Chief."

"I know who it is. What do you want?"

"I'm just leaving the country club, and I noticed something in the green room."

"The green room?"

"That's the small dining room, where you fingerprinted everybody last night."

"OK. What about it?"

"I noticed a spot of what looked like blood on the window blind. Do you know if the crime scene people tested it?"

Butts dropped the receiver on his desk and she heard paper shuffling. After a few moments, he came back on. "Nothing in the file about it. I'll have a word with the tech."

Not a kind word, either, Tess was sure.

"Anything else you want to tell me?"

"No—wait, yes there is. Do you have the medical examiner's report yet?"

"Why do you want to know?" he asked suspiciously.

Tess had her answer ready. "I talked to Raylene Walker today, and she would like to have the body released so she can go ahead with the funeral arrangements."

"The report is in the mail. I talked to the M.E. a little while ago. Julian Walker was stabbed in the heart. Died within seconds. Nothing else unusual."

"Nothing?" Tess mused. For some reason, she felt faintly disappointed.

"Not unless you call an old vasectomy unusual."

"Vasectomy?"

"That's right. Lots of men have them, Tess."

"Of course. Well, thanks, Chief."

Tess disconnected and returned the cell phone to the glove compartment. Turning the air-conditioner fan down a couple of notches, she stared through the windshield as, in the distance, a golf cart stopped at a tee box and two women got out.

She gazed at the women, not really seeing them, as her thoughts dwelt on what she'd just learned. Now she knew what Raylene Walker had lied about. Julian was not the father of the baby Raylene carried. And it now seemed clear that Julian's fury at his wife the evening before had been sparked by the knowledge that another man was the baby's father.

According to Raylene, *He was looking for somebody to blame. I'm sure he wanted to believe I'd been unfaithful. That would have relieved him of any responsibility.* But Julian hadn't merely *wanted* to believe Raylene was unfaithful to relieve himself of responsibility for the child. He'd known for a fact that Raylene was pregnant with another man's child. That was why he'd demanded a divorce, why he'd ordered her to leave the house.

Was it possible Julian hadn't told Raylene about the vasectomy until last night when she'd confronted him with the news of her pregnancy? Perhaps that was what he'd said so quietly that Tess hadn't understood the words.

I don't believe you, Raylene had said. *If it were true, you'd have told me long before now.*

To which Julian had responded, *There was no point. I never expected anything like this to come up. I thought I made that very clear before we married.* Apparently, he'd made it clear that he didn't want children but had failed to tell his wife that he was incapable of fathering a child— until faced with her pregnancy.

If Julian had lived, a divorce would have been inevitable. And Raylene knew that. She'd have been alone with no place to live and no job. Certainly, it had been obvious from her conversation with the other man—the baby's father, Tess realized now—that she could expect no help from him, either.

Tess pulled out of the parking lot, thinking that she should have told Chief Butts that Raylene was pregnant. A small oversight that she would remedy—but not immediately. She wanted time to think about it first and to try to identify the baby's father.

Chapter 15

Back at Iris House, Gertie had left a note on the secretary in Tess's former sitting room, now the new den.

It read: *Chief Butts wants to talk to me tomorrow at eleven. Can you be here?*

Frowning, Tess read it twice with Primrose, her gray Persian, meowing demandingly and winding in and out between her legs. Butts had not mentioned coming to Iris House when she'd phoned him from the club. No doubt he thought it was none of her business. Why did he want to talk to Gertie again? It was worrisome.

She tucked the note into one of the secretary's cubbyholes and went to the kitchen to find a treat for Primrose, who picked it up daintily and carried it away to enjoy at her leisure. Glancing at the kitchen clock, Tess saw that she had barely enough time to get herself ready to go out again.

She was stepping out of the shower when her telephone rang. Wrapping a towel around herself, she left damp footprints on the carpet as she crossed the bedroom to reach the phone.

"Tess? It's Jed Baskin. Kaylynn says you were here to see me this afternoon. Sorry you couldn't wait."

"It wasn't anything urgent, Jed."

"Kaylynn should have let me know you were here. I could've stepped out of my meeting for a minute."

"She seemed sure you didn't want to be disturbed."

He sighed. "She's Helen Qualling's niece." Helen was a long-time member of the country club. "She needed a job and I agreed to give her a try. She's still on probation."

The mystery of Kaylynn's employment was solved. Tess felt obliged to put in a good word for her. "She hasn't had time to get acclimated yet, Jed."

"I know. I'll give her another couple of months. Now, back to what you wanted to see me about. How can I help you?"

"I was just wondering if Julian Walker talked to you shortly before he was killed."

He hesitated, as though the question had surprised him—or given him pause. Then he said thoughtfully, "Let me think. The last time I saw him, he was crossing the patio."

"Entering or exiting the building?"

"He was going in. He didn't speak to me or anyone else that I noticed. He seemed preoccupied. I assumed he was making one last check to see if we needed any more food or drink."

"What time was this, Jed?"

"I can't swear to the time, but it was close to ten, I believe. I remember thinking I should be able to leave for home in another half-hour. I went back to my office, and shortly thereafter, Wayne Trammell came in. We talked for ten or fifteen minutes and were about to leave when we got the news that Julian was dead."

"Have you heard from Raylene Walker today?"

"No, should I have?"

"Not really . . . Jed, there's a rumor going around about Raylene and another man."

"Really? I haven't heard it."

"And I shouldn't be talking about it," Tess said, already

regretting that she had. At least, she now knew that Julian hadn't talked to Jed about the other man before he died. Perhaps he'd gone directly to the other man.

Furthermore, Raylene hadn't gone to the club that afternoon to see Jed. Another unanswered question: Why *had* she gone?

"Forget I told you, Jed."

"Of course." She knew he'd keep his word. Discretion was a prerequisite for any country club manager who expected to enjoy a long tenure.

"Thanks for calling," she said.

"You bet. By the way, Paula's thrilled that you're letting her cater your wedding reception."

"I'm grateful she could take over. I doubt I could have found anybody else on such short notice."

"She said something about an ice sculpture."

"Uh-huh. Paula seemed eager to do it."

"She tried to get Julian to let her do one, but he always insisted on doing them himself. Well, she's certainly taking hold in the kitchen. Otherwise, I'd be searching frantically for a new chef. Now, we can take our time."

"I think Paula hopes you'll offer her the job when she completes her apprenticeship."

Jed chuckled. "She's made that clear—and it's a possibility. Depends on how she works out the next few months."

The conversation ended with Tess thinking that Paula would undoubtedly work out quite well. She was competent, determined, ambitious, and in a position to show off her chef skills—now that Julian was no longer around to keep her under his thumb.

Tess went to her closet and chose a cream silk shirtwaist dress with sage-colored geometric designs scattered over the full skirt. It was one of the outfits Cinny had helped her choose for her trousseau. Maybe it was cheating a little to wear it before the wedding, but she couldn't resist. It was stylish but not too dressy. With her dangly gold hoop earrings, it was perfect for dinner out with Luke and her family.

Her father had made reservations at Ti Amo, an Italian restaurant that had opened less than a year ago. Tess had never eaten there, but she'd heard rave reviews from friends. Tonight, she told herself, she would concentrate on enjoying having her family around her.

But, as she finished dressing, she couldn't help brooding on the fact that Chief Butts wanted to talk to Gertie again.

Tess would take the opportunity to explain to him how Julian's death had placed both Paula Overton and Raylene Walker in very favorable circumstances which they would not have achieved had Julian lived. Butts should be concentrating his investigative efforts on them instead of wasting time on Gertie.

"A toast," Frank Darcy announced, lifting his glass. "To Tess and Luke. May they have many happy years together."

"Hear, hear!"

Champagne glasses clinked.

"And I'd like to toast my family," Tess said, looking around the table with a smile.

"Soon to be my family," Luke put in.

"Thank you for being with us at this important time," Tess went on. "I love you all very much."

More clinking glasses. Zelda had even poured a minute amount of champagne for Madison and Curt to join in the toasts, enough for a couple of swallows each.

Curt made a face. "Don't know why people like that stuff." He grinned at Tess, who was seated beside him at the big, oval table. "I only drank it for Tess."

Tess laughed and mussed his hair. "Thank you for the sacrifice, dear brother." Madison, across the table from Tess, had grimaced at the taste of the champagne, too, but she was in her cool-young-woman-of-the-world mode and not about to admit that she didn't like it or that it was the first time she'd ever tasted champagne. She did look quite grown-up in a figure-hugging red sheath dress, her hair piled atop her head.

"Luke," Madison said now, "where are you going on your honeymoon?"

"Very clever, Maddie," Luke said with a chuckle, "but you didn't catch me off-guard. It's a secret. Not even Tess will know till we're on our way." He was seated on Tess's left and reached for her hand under the table, squeezing it as he spoke.

Madison glanced at Tess and lifted one dark, arched eyebrow. It was an expression that reminded Tess of her Aunt Dahlia. "I can't stand people keeping secrets."

"We know, darling," said Zelda, and everybody laughed, causing Madison to blush prettily.

"Well, it's maddening."

Tess smiled at Luke. "Frankly," she said, "it's one less thing I have to worry about. I'm more than glad to leave the honeymoon plans in Luke's hands. I'm packing for both warm and cold climates."

"But, Tess, what if you don't like the place he picks?" Madison inquired.

"I'm sure I'll love anywhere he chooses."

"The point, Maddie," Frank said, "is for the bride and groom to get away together for a while. The location isn't that important."

Madison tucked a strand of dark hair back into place. "Well, I mean to plan my own honeymoon."

"That's our Madison," Zelda said. "She has to be in control."

Madison frowned at her mother. "What's wrong with that?"

Dahlia, who was seated beside Madison, gave her a hug. "Not a thing, dear. I'm that way myself."

Cinny and Tess exchanged an amused look, and a bark of laughter escaped Maurice. "Why, we never would have guessed, dear," he said.

"A prophet is without honor in her own country," Dahlia retorted. "Pray tell, where would the lot of you be without me?"

"In a complete muddle, I'm sure, darling," Maurice said.

Frank gazed sadly at the remains of his fettucine Alfredo. "Don't know about the rest of you, but I'm stuffed. I can't even finish this delicious meal."

Curt forked the last bite of his cannolini and announced, "I still have room for dessert."

"Naturally," Madison said with a grown-up to grown-ups look around the table. "In case you haven't noticed, Tess, our brother has a bottomless pit for a stomach."

"He's a growing boy," Zelda said with a fond smile for her son. "Frank, would you call the waiter over? We'll see what he has to offer from the dessert tray."

Curt decided on Key lime pie and Maurice chose chocolate-raspberry mousse—so that Curt wouldn't have to eat alone, he said. Everybody else swore he could not hold another bite.

As Curt and Maurice were served dessert, Dahlia said to Tess, "I think I saw Rosa Childress going back there." She indicated the hall where the rest rooms were located. "Please excuse me, everybody. I'll be back in a minute."

"I'll come with you," Tess said and quickly followed her aunt.

Cinny's speculative gaze followed her mother and cousin.

"Who's Rosa Childress?" Frank asked.

"She's in Dahlia's bridge club," Maurice said.

"Oh." Luke looked puzzled.

Cinny pushed back her chair. "Back in a minute," she said, then hurried toward the hall where Dahlia and Tess had just disappeared.

"Now, what are those three up to?" Luke mused.

"You don't want to know," Maurice told him in a resigned voice.

Chapter 16

Tess and Dahlia stood in front of a line of white wash basins when Cinny entered the ladies' room. Dahlia was refreshing her lip gloss as Tess leaned back against one of the basins, waiting. For Cinny's benefit, Tess pointed toward a stall and placed a finger over her lips, cautioning Cinny to be quiet.

Dahlia turned on a tap and washed her hands until Rosa Childress came out of the stall.

"Oh, hello," Rosa greeted them. In her fifties, she had grayed prematurely and now had a beautiful head of platinum-white hair, which was the envy of her friends, who said she could never have achieved such perfection with peroxide. "You all are being awfully quiet," Rosa said as she held her hands under the soap dispenser, then turned on the water.

"We came back here to talk to you, Rosa," Dahlia said.

"Really?" Rosa reached for a paper towel.

"It's about that rumor you heard," Tess said, "the one about Raylene Walker and another man."

Rosa gave Dahlia a disapproving look. "I had hoped what we say at bridge club would remain there."

"I wouldn't have mentioned it," Dahlia said defensively, "if Julian hadn't been killed."

"We think the affair might have some bearing on the murder," Tess added.

"Just tell us the man's name," Cinny inserted, "and we'll make sure the police get the information."

Rosa looked as if she'd tasted something unsavory. "Oh, dear, I don't want any involvement with the police. This whole thing is *so* distasteful, don't you agree?"

"Yes, indeed, and your name will not be mentioned," Dahlia assured her.

Rosa looked vaguely doubtful, "To tell you the truth, I don't know the man's name. The woman who told me just said that Raylene was spending an awful lot of time in the pro shop."

"She's been taking golf lessons," Tess said, feeling deflated.

"I know," Rosa said, "but the way the woman said it, it was clear she thought Raylene was there for another reason."

"Johnny Linzy?" Cinny asked in surprise.

"I never said that!" Rosa insisted.

"Of course, you didn't," Dahlia soothed, "and no one will ever say you did."

Rosa glanced at the faces of the three women before her and seemed satisfied. "It was nice running into you," she said. "Enjoy your evening."

When she left the room, Cinny said, "I've always thought Johnny and Wendy Linzy appeared happily married."

"I don't suppose he'd be the first 'happily married' man to have an affair," Tess mused.

"You know," Dahlia said, "Johnny isn't the only one who works in the pro shop. Don Daily works full time and that young man, Gerald something, works on the weekends."

Don Daily was sixty years old and skinny as a whippet. Gerald hadn't seen his twenty-first birthday yet and had grown so quickly that he was still as awkward as a newborn colt. To Tess, he appeared not to have gotten the hang of manipulating his arms and legs. Tess couldn't see Raylene being interested in either of them.

Of course, Raylene's lover didn't have to be an employee. She could have been meeting a club member in the pro shop.

Still, Paula Overton had said something about a confrontation between Julian and Johnny Linzy the night of the murder. Only it hadn't been over Raylene Walker. It was Johnny who'd told Julian to stay away from his, Johnny's, wife. Could Julian have threatened to inform Wendy of the affair? If so, it certainly gave Johnny Linzy a motive for murder. Was he now worried that Raylene might spill the beans? Could Raylene's life be in danger? Oh, surely, the killer wouldn't risk another murder right away. Still, she should apprise Chief Butts of her suspicions. But she needed hard facts before she gave any of this to the police.

"Let's be careful about naming names," Dahlia said, as if she were reading Tess's thoughts.

"You're right, Aunt Dahlia," Tess agreed. "We can't tell the police anything until we know the man's identity."

"How do you propose to find that out?" Cinny asked.

"I don't know," Tess admitted, but she would think of something. She certainly could not leave on her honeymoon with Gertie still on the police suspect list. Nor could she *not* leave on her honeymoon—in a little less than two weeks now.

All at once, she realized that Raylene's destination that afternoon at the club must have been the pro shop. Had she gone to see Johnny Linzy?

Wendy Linzy finally got her four-year-old son to bed at ten-fifteen. Marcus had really been wired this evening and had begged to stay up past his bedtime. In no mood to deal with a tantrum, Wendy had given in. She sympathized with her son's unwillingness to slip into the unconsciousness of sleep. Though he certainly could not have identified the problem, Marcus, she suspected, felt threatened by his father's extreme distraction during dinner and afterward.

Marcus had pelted Johnny with questions all during the meal and finally, unable to get his father's full attention, had thrown his plate, still containing half his food, on the kitchen floor. Wendy had cleaned up the mess and set her son down in front of a Disney video, hoping to have a conversation with Johnny as they finished their dinner in peace.

But Johnny had pushed his own uneaten meal away and abruptly left the table, saying he had indigestion. He'd poured himself a drink and gone out to the patio, where he sat staring into the distance like one of those film noir anti-heroes freeze-framed on a movie screen, while night, the symbol of life's futility, descended around him. She and Marcus might as well have been on another planet. Frankly, Wendy was getting very tired of Johnny's moods.

Having removed Johnny's plate and put the kitchen to rights, Wendy poured herself a glass of wine and joined her husband on the patio, sliding into the chair next to his. "We need to talk," she said without preamble.

Johnny sat forward and rubbed both hands down his face. She recognized the signs of dismissal. Afraid he was going to say he was too tired to talk and was going to bed, she hurried on.

"It's about us."

"Us?" His voice was careful, noncommittal.

"If there's someone else, Johnny, I'd rather you just tell me straight. I can't stand all this brooding."

"What makes you think there's someone else?"

Wendy was vastly relieved to hear that he sounded surprised and chose to interpret this as a positive sign.

"Lately, when you're at home, your mind is far from here."

While she'd bathed Marcus and put him to bed, she had run through her mind all the possible reasons for Johnny's withdrawal from her of late. The most frightening, and thus the one she'd decided to attack head on, was that he had fallen in love with somebody else. But she'd given him an opening to tell her, and he wasn't going to take it. Which didn't prove he hadn't been playing around; but it seemed clear he didn't want to break up his marriage over it.

"I hope you're not listening to gossip. You know how some of those women at the club are. Flirtation is their middle name. It means nothing."

What gossip? Wendy wondered, but she wasn't ready to badger him on that point. If he told her, she might have to do something about it. She wished she could see his face better; his expression might give her a clue. But, even though the yard lamps were on, they sat in the shadow of the patio roof.

"I can handle being ignored, but it infuriates Marcus when he can't get your attention. I thought I'd never get him to bed."

"I'm sorry . . . I'm not feeling very well."

She sighed. "That's not good enough, Johnny. I want to know what's really wrong."

"There's no reason for me to unload my problems on you. You'd just worry, and you can't do anything about it."

"I'm your wife, Johnny. I want to be a full partner in your life—all of it."

"No you don't," he said bitterly.

It angered her that he could dismiss her concerns so flatly. She reached out and gripped his shoulder, trying to make him look at her. "Not knowing, constantly worrying, is worse than whatever's turned you into a stranger in your own house. What's *wrong*, dammit!"

He grabbed her wrist, flung her hand away. He turned his head and stared before them, into the darkness. "Leave me alone."

Coming to her feet, she stood in front of him. "No! Look at me! Talk to me!"

He said nothing for a long moment. He still wore the shirt and shorts he'd worn all day at the club, another sign that things weren't right. He usually showered and changed as soon as he hit the door. Now he placed his hands on his bare knees and, even in the shadows, she could see them gripped so tightly that his knuckles must be white. Then he leaned forward, putting his face in better light. A muscle worked like a spasm in his jaw.

"How would you feel about leaving here?"

"Here? You mean selling the house." She loved their house, but something told her she was fighting for her marriage now. She forced herself to say, "If you really think the house is too big, if it bothers you that much, then we can talk about selling."

"I'm not talking about the house. I want to leave this town. There are plenty of other pro jobs."

His pinched features manifested the misery of a man who felt trapped. So there was another woman, after all. A part of her could even understand his yielding to temptation, the way some of those women at the club threw themselves at him. Wendy had always suspected that half the women who took golf lessons weren't as interested in improving their game as they were in spending time with her husband. But at least he wanted to run away from the other woman, and he wanted Wendy and Marcus to go with him.

Was the other woman, if there was one, pressuring him to leave his family? Perhaps threatening to talk to Wendy herself?

"If you still love me, Johnny, whatever you've done, we can work through it."

He stared at her for a long moment before pushing himself slowly to his feet. "You have no idea what you're saying," he said heavily. He sounded utterly hopeless.

Wendy felt frustration rising like steam escaping from her chest to burn her throat. He was treating her like a child who could not comprehend the matters adults grappled with. Exactly as her father treated her sometimes, she realized suddenly. But she tolerated her father's overprotectiveness because she could use it to get what she wanted. She would not, however, put up with it from her husband.

She stood, moving to block his way into the house. Taking his face in both hands, she forced him to look at her. "Then explain it to me!"

For a moment, she thought she'd gotten through to him, that he would tell her, finally, what was wrong. But what he said was, "There are some things your father's money can't buy us out of."

"Johnny . . ."

He clasped her wrists to remove her hands from his face, then, gripping her waist, he lifted her easily and set her aside. "No," he said and he went into the house, leaving her standing there, defeated, frustration threatening to explode her chest.

Chapter 17

"Chief Butts told me he'd received some new information that he needed to talk to me about," Gertie said the next morning as she and Tess waited in the guest parlor for Butts's scheduled arrival.

Tess had explained the situation to her family and the Stedmans, saying that she would appreciate their staying out of sight until after the chief had come and gone.

"I can't imagine what new information he'd need to talk to you about," Tess said now.

"Me, either." Nervously, Gertie wadded her apron skirt in both hands. "He just said he'd made some phone calls, but when I asked what it had to do with me, he hung up."

How like Butts to set up a situation where the other person was on the defensive before the interview even started. "The chief enjoys dangling these little tidbits in front of people to put them off-guard."

"Well, he's scaring me spitless," Gertie wailed. "He's got it in for me."

"If this harassment continues," Tess said, "we might want to think about getting Cody Yount to represent you." Cody was an up-and-coming trial lawyer who, recently, had successfully defended a local merchant charged with the murder of a family member.

"Cody Yount!" Gertie yelped, looking even more alarmed. "Do you really think I need a lawyer?"

"Personally, Gertie, I can't believe Chief Butts has enough to charge you with anything," Tess said, as calmly and soothingly as she could manage. "But if you had representation, you could refer all Butts's questions to Cody."

"Maybe you're right," Gertie conceded.

Glancing out the window, Tess saw Butts's patrol car pull up. "He's here."

Gertie wadded her apron again while Tess went to the front door to admit the chief.

Butts lumbered past Tess and into the parlor. "Miz Bogart," he said without preamble, "I've got a little bad news for you."

"Bad news?" Gertie queried anxiously.

Butts cleared his throat portentously. "I called that food company, the one that ran the contest where you say Julian Walker cheated you out of fifty grand."

Gertie exchanged a puzzled look with Tess, who now sat beside her on the green velvet Victorian love seat. Tess wanted Butts to face a united front.

"Got the names of a couple of the judges and ran them down," Butts went on as he pulled his tablet from his uniform pocket. He looked up. "Do you remember what you said to Walker?"

"I imagine I said a lot of things," Gertie admitted.

"According to my sources, you told Walker, in the hearing of at least two judges, that you'd make him pay for what he'd done if it took the rest of your life."

Gertie went white.

"What," Tess demanded, "does that have to do with Julian's murder?"

"Seems obvious to me," Butts told her.

"I was angry. I—didn't mean I'd kill him," Gertie croaked, her capable hands twisting together in her lap. "I *never* meant anything like that."

"Of course she didn't," Tess put in.

"Exactly what did you have in mind then?" Butts asked. "How did you plan to make him pay?"

"I wrote to the head of the food company and to the Chefs of America board and told them what Julian Walker had done."

"According to the judges I talked to, there was never any evidence that Walker was the one who put the salt in your sugar."

"Oh, he made sure of that," Gertie said bitterly.

"So by making him pay, you meant you'd write a couple of letters?" Butts asked with obvious disbelief.

"Yes. I wanted it on his record, even if they did nothing about it."

"Which they didn't," Butts said.

"I guess not," Gertie agreed.

"They thought you were just a sore loser," Butts goaded. "Said it happened all the time in those cooking contests."

Color flushed Gertie's face. "I can't help what they thought."

Butts studied Gertie for a long moment, scowling. "Miz Bogart, if there's anything else you need to tell me, now's the time."

Gertie bristled. "I've told you everything I know about the murder."

"I get it. That's your story and you're sticking to it."

"Chief," Tess said, "she's told you all she knows."

Butts turned to a clean page in his tablet. "Let's go over your story again. Start from when you walked into the country club kitchen and saw Walker for the first time in two years."

Gertie did so, haltingly at first, then with more vigor and determination, with Tess adding a few minor details that Gertie omitted, none of them significant. It was the same narrative, in all important details, as what she'd told Butts before. When Gertie finished, Butts tucked his notebook back in his pocket. He seemed disgruntled, probably because Gertie hadn't slipped up and incriminated herself.

"I'll get this typed up," he said shortly. "I'm gonna need you to come down to the station tomorrow and sign your statement."

Gertie, on the verge of tears, gazed at Tess, who patted her hand consolingly and followed Butts into the foyer, where he walked through red, yellow, and green pools of light on the flagstone floor, made by sunlight shining through the stained glass door panes.

"Chief," Tess demanded, as soon as they were out of the parlor, "why are you badgering Gertie?"

He looked at her in feigned surprise that she could ask a question with such an obvious answer. "I'm just putting a little pressure on a suspect. It's a routine investigative technique."

Tess wanted to hit him. While he was "pressuring" Gertie, the trail to the real murderer was getting cold. "Has the lab had a chance to check that blood spot on the window blind in the green room?"

He stared at her consideringly, then said, "It's Walker's blood type. We won't get the DNA results for several weeks. In the meantime, we can assume it's Walker's blood. We needed to know about that spot, for the sake of being thorough, but it's not exactly a case-breaking clue."

"It tells you Walker was stabbed in the dining room and then removed to the pantry, doesn't it?"

"Probably. So what?"

"There was no blood anywhere else in the green room."

"Puzzling, I'll admit."

"The blood on the blind indicates it spurted out when Walker was stabbed," Tess mused. She had convinced herself of this because it seemed unlikely the murderer would have touched the closed blinds after the murder. He'd have been desperate to get away.

"The killer must've immediately moved the body. I

haven't figured out how he did it yet. We know he didn't drag it because there were no marks on the carpet."

"The blood must've gotten on the killer's clothes."

A wicked glow lit the chief's eyes. "The only person with blood on her clothes was Miz Bogart."

"Only one smear and she explained that. She touched Walker to see if he was dead. When she got to the kitchen doorway, she realized she had blood on her hand and swiped it down her dress. Aunt Dahlia, Cinny, and I all saw her do that."

"Are you sure the blood wasn't already on the dress, and she just pretended to wipe it there once she got where the three of you could see her?"

"I'm sure. Gertie was practically in shock, Chief. She wasn't thinking clearly enough to stage something like that."

"There was no blood on anybody else I talked to that night," Butts said stubbornly.

"Then somehow the murderer got away before Uncle Maurice rounded up the stragglers."

"A nice little theory, Tess, but you got no evidence to back it up."

"We know that Raylene Walker left shortly before the body was discovered. Are you putting pressure on her, too?"

He shrugged. "I've talked to her. Talked to a couple of other people, too—people Maurice Forrest said he saw leaving about the same time as Raylene Walker. They didn't know anything."

"Have you searched Raylene's house?"

"Don't think I could get a warrant. Anyway, it would probably be a waste of time. If she had any incriminating evidence around, she'd have gotten rid of it by now."

"There may have been others you don't know about who left the club about the same time Raylene did. I'll see if anybody you questioned at the country club saw others leaving."

His expression told her he thought she was grasping at straws. "If you get any names, I can have Officer Neill talk to them, but don't expect anything to come of it. Those bloody clothes, if they ever existed, have been destroyed by now." He seemed determined to believe there were no bloody clothes around, other than Gertie's.

"Something else you need to know," Tess said. "Raylene Walker is pregnant."

He rocked back on his heels. The revelation left him speechless, but only for a moment. "Her old man was shooting blanks, so he couldn't have knocked her up. Who's the daddy?"

"Whoever she's having an affair with. I'm trying to find out who that is."

"Well, be careful how you go about it, Tess. And you let me know if you find out."

"You can count on it. Chief, Julian Walker went outside that night to talk to somebody. Jed Baskin says Julian didn't talk to him."

"If Baskin is telling the truth."

"Yes," Tess agreed, "and if so Julian could've talked to the other man. If Julian threatened to reveal the affair—to the man's wife, perhaps—it sure gives that man a motive for murder."

"And Raylene Walker's still pregnant," Butts pointed out. "How can he be sure *she* won't tell?"

"For all we know, she has told him she won't."

"Maybe I'll caution her to watch her back," Butts mused.

"She obviously doesn't know that you discovered Julian had had a vasectomy," Tess said. "She's saying it's her husband's baby."

"Hmm. We'll keep that little secret between the two of us for now, OK? I'll let Miz Walker know I know about the vasectomy when the time is right."

Tess nodded, and Butts went on, "But I have to tell you, Tess, that your cook is still the best suspect I've turned up."

"That is too ridiculous!"

He chuckled sarcastically. "Yeah, yeah. I admire your loyalty, Tess. But try to put yourself in my shoes." He ticked off his evidence on his fingers. "One, I got Miz Bogart's thumb print on the murder weapon. Two, she threatened to make Julian Walker pay for cheating her out of that cooking prize."

"That was two years ago!"

"Two years when she didn't have access to the victim—until the other night. Now, where was I?" He stared at the two fingers he was holding up. "Oh, yeah, number three, she had blood on her dress, and, four, she's the one who discovered the body." He held the four fingers in Tess's face as if to make her acknowledge that the evidence against Gertie was irrefutable.

"Then tell me how a middle-aged woman moved a body from the green room to the pantry without help."

"She's a pretty big woman, Tess."

"But Julian was no pygmy, either. Gertie doesn't have the strength to move a man the size of Julian Walker."

"Sometimes, in a crisis, adrenaline gives people the strength to do stuff they could never do otherwise. I know a case where an average-sized man moved a car off his wife after it fell from a jack on her, and another where a woman who couldn't swim a lick jumped in a lake and brought her two-year-old child back to shore."

He had an answer for every argument she put forth, and at the moment Tess could not think of anything else to offer in Gertie's defense.

"Tess," Butts added, and a cajoling note had come into his tone, "Miz Bogart trusts you. You could get her to confide in you. Tell her the truth always comes out in the end."

Tess was so frustrated that she stamped her foot. "She's already confided in me—and in you! Gertie did not kill that man!"

Butts sighed, as if giving up on Tess as a hopeless case. "Lord, you are a comfort, Tess. Now, I gotta get back to the station. Call me if you stumble over any real evidence on anybody else."

Chapter 18

After rescheduling a fitting session for her bridal gown following Butts's second interrogation of Gertie, Tess spent the afternoon phoning the people whom Maurice had brought into the club dining room for questioning the night of the murder. None of them remembered seeing anybody leaving shortly before the body was discovered. They'd been busy talking to friends and hadn't really been paying attention to who was leaving.

This didn't prove that it didn't happen. The parking lot was on one side of the building and not visible from the patio in back, where most of the people she talked to had been. Still, Tess was disappointed. She had to come up with something to prove Gertie's innocence, and the only thing that would convince Chief Butts was indisputable evidence on the real murderer.

Sitting at the desk in her office, she took out a piece of paper and wrote "Suspects" and "Motives" at the top. Then she listed the following:

Raylene Walker   *Julian threatened to put her out on the street.*

Paula Overton   *Julian threatened to fire her*

Raylene's lover   *Raylene was pregnant with his child and*
                      Julian threatened to expose him

Tess paused and chewed the end of her pen for a moment,
thinking. Who else might have wanted Julian dead? She
wrote one last name.

Craig Young   *Known to have a hot temper and had*
                      resorted to violence before. Over-
                      heard saying nobody talked to him as
                      Julian did and got away with it.

Desperately wanting to do *something*, Tess looked under
"Young" in the telephone book. Like many teenagers,
Craig Young had his own private telephone line. He was
listed at the same address on Ash Avenue as C. T. and
Carma Young.

She would probably learn nothing new by talking to
him, but anything was worth a try. And she wanted to see
Craig's face when she did it. Luke had invited her family
over that evening for a cookout, but she had enough time to
drop in on Craig before that.

Grabbing her purse, she left her quarters and almost ran
into Madison in the foyer. "Going somewhere?" Tess
asked.

"No, I'm tired of reading, so I was coming to visit you."

"I have to go out."

"Can I go with you?" Madison asked eagerly, then
glanced down at her brief denim shorts and red halter top.
"I can change if you want me to."

Tess's first impulse was to deny Madison's request, but
on second thought, Craig Young might be more willing to
talk to Tess if her pretty, fifteen-year-old sister were present.

"You're fine," Tess said, "but go upstairs and tell your
mother we're going to run an errand. We should be back in
a half-hour."

On the drive to the Youngs' address, Tess explained her real purpose in going there.

Madison's expressive eyes grew wide. "This Craig is a murder suspect? Oh, wow, how exciting."

"He's not very high on the suspect list," Tess admitted, "but I wanted to talk to him to see if he noticed anything that night that might relate to the murder."

"Why doesn't Chief Butts talk to him?"

"The chief is concentrating on Gertie."

"Gertie! You mean he came here to talk to her today because he thinks she stabbed that man?"

"Apparently that's what he thinks."

"That's insane! Gertie is not a murderer." Her reaction was the same as that of everybody who knew Gertie—all except Chief Butts.

"So I keep telling the chief, but I don't think I'm getting through his hard head."

Driving the next few blocks in silence, Tess realized that her wedding was only ten days away now. Ten days in which she had to clear Gertie of Julian Walker's murder. The modest but well-maintained neighborhood through which they passed was clean and bright, in contrast to Tess's darkly anxious mood. Pristine windows caught the afternoon sunlight, hedges were trimmed to perfection, and riots of color spilled from flower beds.

The Young house, an old bungalow with a wide front porch, sported a new coat of white paint. Like its neighbors, it was well-maintained, with aluminum awnings—white with green stripes—across the front, and red impatiens blooming in a bed beside the front steps.

Craig was mowing the front lawn when Tess and Madison drove up. He stopped and turned off the motor as the two of them got out of the car and walked toward him. He wore thongs and a pair of shorts. Sweat glistened on his face and tanned chest and arms. He pulled a handkerchief from his hip pocket and wiped his face, his gaze fixed on Madison.

"He's cute," Madison whispered to Tess.

"Don't even think about it," Tess murmured.

"What, you believe I'd go out with a murder suspect?"

Tess had no chance to answer, as they were now within feet of Craig. "Sorry to interrupt your work," Tess said.

"I was ready for a break," Craig told her, his eyes returning to Madison. He smiled. "Hi. Do you live in Victoria Springs?"

"I live in Paris—France." Craig looked suitably impressed by this.

"Craig, this is my sister, Madison Darcy," Tess said. "She's here for my wedding."

"I'm helping Tess get ready," Madison told him. "You wouldn't believe how much there is to do for a formal wedding. I'm busy from morning till night."

Tess glanced askance at her sister, the sister who had spent the afternoon reading. Madison was certainly not busy, but perhaps it was her way of rebuffing a date before it was offered.

"I'm helping Chief Butts interview the people who were at the club the night Julian Walker was murdered," Tess improvised, and she ignored Madison's surprised look.

"I already talked to him," Craig said.

"I know, but he wants to see if you've remembered anything else since then."

"Like what?"

"Like seeing somebody leave the club shortly before Maurice Forrest came and asked you and Jeff to go to the dining room to meet with the police."

"People had been leaving the barbecue for an hour. I can't remember who left last. I wasn't paying that much attention. I was helping Paula clean up."

"Did you happen to notice anybody with stains on their clothes?"

He looked bewildered. "Stains, like barbecue sauce?"

"Like blood," Tess said.

"Oh." He scratched his chin. "Nope, sorry. It was pretty

dark by then." He stretched his arms out and curled his hands into fists, as if working a kink out of a muscle. It was also a way to flex his well-developed pecs and biceps—for Madison's benefit.

Madison slid a sideways glance in Tess's direction. She was not impressed.

Tess had a new thought. "Did you notice anybody wearing different clothes from the ones they'd had on when the barbecue started? Think hard, Craig. It's important."

He did appear to think hard for a long moment, then said, "I see what you're getting at. You think maybe the murderer got blood on his clothes and had to change."

"Right."

"Sorry, wish I could help, but I didn't see anybody like that and I probably would have. I know most guys wouldn't, but I usually notice what people are wearing." His eyes raked Madison's brief apparel, and it was clear he liked what he saw. In an uncharacteristic self-conscious gesture, Madison folded her arms across her chest.

As for Tess, she was feeling more deflated than ever. Hoping to learn of someone who'd changed clothes in the middle of the evening had been an off-the-wall idea, anyway, she admitted. For somebody to have brought a change of clothes with them, he'd have had to know he was going to murder Julian and might need them. But there didn't appear to have been any planning; everything pointed to an impulse murder.

Tess decided to play her last card. "I know Julian was rough on you and Jeff that night."

"He was a bas—" He paused, looked sheepishly at Madison. "He was a jerk."

"You were overheard saying that nobody treated you that way and got away with it," Tess said.

Her trump card didn't seem to bother him in the least. "Yeah, I might've said that. I don't like people dissing me. And I might've taken a punch at the guy if somebody else hadn't killed him first. He deserved a punch in the face for the way he was acting that night."

"Did he deserve to be murdered?"

"Naw, he just needed taking down a notch."

The meeting had been a waste of time, and standing in the hot sun, Tess was beginning to perspire. "I'll tell Chief Butts you haven't remembered anything else since he talked to you. Thanks for your time, Craig."

"No problem," Craig said and, then, as Madison and Tess turned to go, "Say, Madison, do you think you might have time for a movie or something while you're here?"

Madison arranged her face into an expression of disappointment. Her sister, Tess realized, was a consummate actress. "I'm awfully sorry, Craig, but I know I won't. It's sweet of you to ask, though."

"When will you be coming back to town?" Craig persisted.

"I've no idea."

Back in the car, Madison said, "Ugh, I didn't like him at all. He's as cocky as a bantam rooster."

Cocky enough to believe he could get away with murder? Tess wondered. She wanted to believe it, but, as much as she wanted to exonerate Gertie, she had a hard time seeing Craig Young as the killer. In the past, he'd solved his problems with his fists. Taking a punch at Julian was much more in keeping with what she knew of him.

"You handled his invitation in a very mature manner," Tess said.

Maddie shrugged. "No reason to hurt his feelings."

Chapter 19

With sundown, a soft breeze came up, making Luke's backyard a pleasant setting for the meal he had prepared, which featured grilled steaks and barbecued pork ribs. All of Tess's relatives were in attendance, along with Cody Yount. It was a relaxing evening, filled with laughter and convivial conversation. It would have been perfect if Tess hadn't been so worried about Gertie.

"Tess, you are very fortunate to be marrying such a good cook," Zelda said halfway through the meal.

"Maurice can cook, too," Dahlia put in, "but after we married I could never get him to enter the kitchen unless a meal was on the table."

"He didn't have to impress you after the ceremony," Cinny said, grinning at her father.

Tess looked lovingly at her fiance. "I'll take Luke, even if he won't cook."

"Ahhh, love," said Curt.

"Your turn's coming, Curt," Luke told him.

"Are there any more ribs?" Frank asked. He'd already filled his plate twice.

Zelda looked pointedly at the pile of rib bones on his plate. "You're going to make yourself sick, dear."

"Yeah, but it'll be worth it," Frank retorted, causing

everybody to laugh. "You can't get ribs like this in Paris."

Luke got up to scoop ribs from the grill with a big ladle. "This is the last batch. Who else wants ribs?"

Maurice and Curt spoke up, and Luke distributed the ribs among the three. Dahlia and Zelda exchanged a look of futility—trying to talk their men into calling on a little self-discipline was useless.

Gnawing on his last rib bone, Curt asked, "What's for dessert?"

"Tess brought some pies," Luke informed him.

"Cherry and apple. They're not homemade," Tess confessed. "But they're from the Victoria Springs Bakery, and pies are their specialty."

"Nobody expects you to bake pies," Dahlia told her, "not with everything else you have to do."

Tess got up to go to the kitchen and bring out the pies and dessert plates, but Dahlia forestalled her. "I'll do it, Tess. I'm sure you've been running around all day."

Tess, who was seated beside Luke and across the table from Cinny and Cody, was perfectly willing to let Dahlia play hostess. "There's ice cream in the freezer," Tess called to her aunt, "for those who want it à la mode."

Tess had wanted to speak to Cody about Gertie all evening, and as the others had fallen into conversation at another table, now seemed a good time.

"Cody, Chief Butts came back to Iris House this morning to question Gertie again."

Cody's eyes turned grave. "A second time?"

Tess nodded. "Did you hear what he said to her?" Cody asked.

"Every word. Gertie wanted me to stay with her. Do you know about the cooking contest Gertie took part in with Julian Walker a couple of years ago?"

"Cinny told me," Cody said.

"Well, Butts had talked to two of the judges, who told him that Gertie threatened to make Walker pay for cheating her out of the prize."

"Poo," Cinny said indignantly, passing this off with a flick of her fingers. "That's not a convincing motive for murder."

"No, it isn't," Cody agreed.

"My guess is," Luke said, "that Butts has no promising suspects, or at least no good evidence on anybody, so he's zeroed in on Gertie."

"You're exactly right," Tess said. "He had the nerve to say if there was anything else Gertie wanted to tell him, she should get on with it."

Cinny heaved a disgusted sigh. "Did he actually expect her to confess to murder?"

"I don't know, but Gertie is scared to death. Cody, I suggested she might want to get legal representation if the chief keeps this up."

"Absolutely," Cody agreed. "I'll be happy to be her buffer with Butts at no cost—unless things change significantly."

"Good," Tess said, feeling relieved. "Thank you, Cody. I'm sure Gertie will feel much better if you can deal with the police for her."

"Tell her next time the chief wants to talk, she should refer him to me."

"She has to go down to the station tomorrow and sign her statement."

"What time?"

"About ten. I'm going with her."

"I'll have to check my calendar, but I think I can meet you there."

"You're a lifesaver, Cody."

Cinny giggled. "I'd like to see the chief's face when Cody shows up. He still hasn't gotten over that murder case Cody won last year because the police were so careless with evidence that it got thrown out." She reached for Cody's hand and laced her fingers through his, beaming at him proudly. "Cody had Butts on the stand for over an hour. He made the whole police force look pretty inept."

"In that particular case," Cody said, "they were inept. It was just a matter of informing the jury of the many mistakes they made. Besides, my client was innocent."

"Don't all your clients claim they're innocent?" Luke inquired.

"Most of them, but this time it was true. I proved that to the jury's satisfaction."

Tess hoped, if Butts actually convinced the D.A. to put Gertie on trial, that Cody could do as well for her. She admitted to herself what she had yet to mention to Luke. If the case wasn't resolved and somebody besides Gertie wasn't charged before the wedding, she and Luke would have to delay their honeymoon. She simply could not leave Gertie alone to face a murder charge.

Luke turned to her. "You can stop worrying so much now, darling. Let Cody do the worrying."

"I'll try," Tess said, "but it's difficult, seeing Gertie so tense all the time. Butts said putting the pressure on a suspect was a routine investigative technique, but it still makes me mad enough to do the man bodily harm. I suggested she take a couple of days off, but she won't."

She must, Tess told herself, let Luke know before the evening ended how she felt about leaving on their honeymoon if Gertie was still in trouble.

As it turned out, Luke's reaction was all that Tess could have hoped for. She told him on the drive to Iris House. "Of course," he said, "we can't leave Gertie in the lurch."

"If you've made a deposit on a trip, you may have to forfeit it," Tess said.

"It's only money, and not such a big amount, at that. Standing by Gertie is more important than a few dollars."

Tess snuggled next to him and rested her head on his shoulder. "You are such a dear. No wonder I'm madly in love with you."

He took his eyes off the dark, deserted street long enough to give her a quick kiss. "We'll have our honeymoon, sweetheart. It may be delayed, but that's not a serious problem. Sidney can take over for me whenever I need him."

"Is he still excited about moving into your house?" Luke's office, where he managed his clients' money and invested their portfolios, was in his home, and he'd asked his assistant, Sidney Lawson, if he was interested in moving in when Luke moved to Iris House. Sidney had jumped at the chance and had immediately started rearranging furniture. Luke had had to remind Sidney that he wasn't gone yet.

"You could say that," Luke said, chuckling. "He's marking off the days until the wedding on a calendar beside his desk."

"Well, he is in that tiny apartment." Tess had gone there once with Luke. "There's hardly room to turn around."

"So he tells me at least once a day. To listen to him, you'd think he was barely scraping by. But I offer no sympathy. I'm paying Sidney enough for him to afford a bigger place. He's a miser. Says he's going to be a millionaire before he's forty."

Tess knew that the rent Luke had asked for the roomy space he was moving out of was far less than he could get on the open market. "Sidney is lucky to have such a considerate employer," she murmured.

"It's worth it to me to have somebody I trust living there." They had reached Iris House, and Luke parked at the curb. "Are you too tired for me to come in for a while?"

"I would love for you to come in," Tess told him. "In fact, I can't wait for you to be here all the time. But I suppose we'd better wait until after the wedding for that."

"I know. Zelda doesn't want us to set a bad example for her kids."

Tess laughed as they got out of the car. His arm around her, they walked slowly up the front walk. "Zelda is under the illusion that she has protected her precious innocents from the ways of the world."

A bark of laughter escaped Luke. "Curt, maybe. But our Maddie? I fear Zelda is deluded."

They stepped into the foyer and Tess got out her key to open the door to her quarters. "You're right, but I don't think Zelda has to worry about Maddie. She can take care of herself. You should have seen the way she handled Craig Young today."

"Craig Young?"

"I'll tell you about it later," Tess said as Luke closed the door behind them, shutting them in with the darkness.

Taking her in his arms, he whispered into her hair, "Our time is limited, so let's make the best of it."

Chapter 20

As good as his word, Cody was waiting outside the police station the next morning when Tess and Gertie arrived. They went in together and Cody introduced himself to the officer at the desk, adding "My client, Mrs. Bogart, is here to sign a statement."

The young officer went in search of Chief Butts, who stomped in shortly, looking like a thundercloud and carrying several pieces of paper covered with typing—clearly Gertie's statement. He eyed Cody with chagrin. "People who hire lawyers before they're charged with anything usually have something to hide."

"You know better than that, Chief," Cody responded good-naturedly. "Mrs. Bogart isn't used to dealing with the police and asked me to guide her through the process."

"Yeah, right," Butts snarled. He thrust the papers at Gertie. "Here's the transcript of your statement. Read it carefully before you sign. I don't want any recantations later."

"Why would I recant?" Gertie asked. "There's nothing incriminating here—not if you put it down like I told you." She sat down to read the statement, and Tess took the chief aside to say, "I have an idea who the father of Raylene Walker's baby is. He's the one you should be going after."

"Still telling me how to do my job, eh, Tess? Well, give me his name and I'll talk to him."

Tess hesitated. Butts was likely to blunder in like a bull in a china closet, and the man's defenses would go up all over the place. "At this point, it's just a rumor. I'd rather confirm my suspicion before it goes any further."

Butts's face got red. "If you screw up my investigation, I'll charge you with obstruction."

"If you wish to charge me with anything," Tess retorted, "speak to my attorney."

Butts glanced at Cody, who stood beside Gertie's chair, reading over her shoulder. "Yount, I presume."

"Correct."

"You get lawyers involved, Tess, and everything gets a lot more complicated. They like to file motions with the court."

"It's their job."

"Hmph," Butts said disdainfully.

After consulting with Cody, Gertie signed the statement and handed it to Butts. As they left the station, Cody said, "Chief, I've advised my client not to talk to you again unless I'm present. So if you have any further business with her, you know how to reach me."

Mumbling under his breath, Butts stomped back to his office without reply.

"He's not a happy camper," Tess observed.

"It's not my goal to make him happy," Cody said.

"I'll tell you one thing," Gertie put in, "*I* felt a lot better, having you there looking out for my interests."

After delivering Gertie back to Iris House, Tess went for the final fitting of her bridal gown. By the time she left the seamstress's house, it was well after noon, so she stopped for a salad at Harry's Grill. After lunch, she had several more stops to make, one of them at Cinny's bookshop, where Cinny helped her pick out gift books and silver bookmarks for Maddie, the friend she'd asked to attend to the guest book, and those who would serve at the reception. That took care of all the attendants except for Cinny, and she'd already purchased Cinny's gift, a beautifully embroidered cosmetic case for traveling.

Tess signed gift cards for Cinny to tuck into the packages before she wrapped them.

"I'll pick them up next week sometime," Tess said as she left the shop.

Dusk was falling as she returned, famished, to Iris House. She warmed up a leftover casserole for a quick dinner. She still hadn't found the time to confront the man she suspected was Raylene Walker's lover. He should be at home by now, she thought, as she decided to try to set up an appointment with him.

His wife answered, and when Tess asked to speak to Johnny, Wendy said, "He walked back to the club after dinner. Said he had a late meeting."

"I'll try him later."

"May I ask who's calling?"

Tess hung up without identifying herself. She would prefer to talk to Johnny Linzy at the club anyway, and there was no time like the present.

The pro shop was closed, but Tess could see Johnny through the glass door, bending over a counter. He appeared to be just staring into space. She tapped on the pane. He looked up, then came to open the door for her.

"Can I help you, Tess?"

"I'm sorry to interrupt your work, but it's important that I talk to you."

"I'm not really working, and you sound very serious," he said, frowning. "Come on in. We can talk in my office."

"Your wife said you had a late meeting."

"It's over," he said shortly. He was dressed in his usual working attire, walking shorts and a knit shirt with the club logo on the pocket. There was a rack of the shirts in several colors in the pro shop. His handsome face looked strained. Lines she hadn't noticed before were carved in parentheses from his nose to the corners of his mouth, and there were dark smudges around his eyes. He turned to the credenza behind his desk, where a half-full coffeemaker sat, a red light shining on its stand. He poured himself a cup and turned to Tess, coffee pot still in hand. "Care for a cup?"

"No, thanks. It's too late for me," Tess said. "Keeps me awake."

He added a heaping spoonful of sugar and stirred. His gestures seemed agitated. "Me, too."

"Are you trying to stay awake for some reason?"

"God, no. I wish I could sleep for a week." Whatever the cause, he didn't appear to have been sleeping well for some time.

Seated across the desk from him in the small office, Tess decided to use an approach that had worked for her before, stating as fact something she only suspected.

"I'll get right to the point, Johnny. I've talked to Raylene Walker and I know she's pregnant with your child."

He seemed frozen for a moment, then slowly set his coffee cup down. He raked a hand through his hair and adjusted his waistband, as though gathering himself together. "I can't believe Raylene said a thing like that, so you can't possibly know it."

"Raylene says Julian is the father."

His taut face muscles visibly relaxed, but his blue eyes looked to be made of flint. "Then, if I were you, I wouldn't go around spreading lies."

"The lie is that Julian is the father," Tess told him. "The autopsy revealed that Julian had undergone a vasectomy."

She could see he was surprised by this, but he shrugged, an attempt at nonchalance. "If Raylene tries to pin it on me, I'll deny it with my last breath. It's my word against hers."

"Except that a DNA test when the child is born could

prove it. Furthermore, you've been seen with her." This was stretching it a bit, but Tess was not above telling a few white lies in aid of providing Chief Butts with a more probable suspect than Gertie.

"Where? By whom?"

"I'd rather not reveal that yet. I'll just say that a country club is like a very small town. Sooner or later, everybody knows everybody else's business."

He fidgeted in his chair, reached for his coffee cup, changed his mind, and let his hand drop. "Look, Tess. Supposing what you say were true—and I'm not admitting anything—what purpose would be served by coming out with it now? Whatever relationship I had with Raylene is over."

It was an admission of sorts, but one that he would probably deny in front of anyone else.

"The night of the barbecue, Julian confronted you about Raylene's pregnancy, didn't he?"

"So that's it? God, what a mess." He slumped forward in his chair and dropped his head to his hands, his fingers splayed out on either side of his face. "I told him to keep his voice down, but he was beyond reasoning with. I've been hoping nobody took any notice of what he was saying. Julian was often in a stew about something." He lifted his gaze to Tess's face and added in a monotone, "Raylene had just told Julian she was pregnant, and he had apparently heard a rumor about me and Raylene. It still doesn't prove I'm the father of that child."

"Did he threaten to go to Jed?"

"No, he said he was going to tell Wendy. I warned him to stay away from my wife."

"And then he was murdered. And now, if harm should come to Raylene, you'll be the prime suspect."

He straightened up and gripped the edge of his desk with both hands. "What are you saying, Tess? You can't possibly believe I killed Julian or that I'd hurt Raylene."

"What I believe isn't important, is it? It's what the police will believe."

"*Will* believe? You haven't told them about me and Raylene yet, have you?" His tone took on an urgency. "Tess, I swear to you I did not kill Julian Walker. And I beg you not to go to the police with this. Wendy knows nothing about Raylene. If she learns of that now, my marriage could be over."

"Perhaps you should tell her yourself, before she hears it from someone else."

Anger flared in his eyes. He turned to stare out the window at evening shadows. "I'm afraid to. I don't want to lose my wife and son. Surely you can understand that."

"Then you should go to the police and tell them exactly what happened that night before Julian was killed."

"Nothing happened! Julian stormed up to me and said he was going to tell Wendy that I'd been having an affair with his wife and that she was pregnant with my child and I should be prepared to support the baby for the next eighteen years. Wendy and I disagree about money matters as it is. How do you think she'd react to having to pay child support for eighteen years?"

He should have thought of that before he made Raylene pregnant, Tess thought. "That's hardly the point, Johnny. If it comes to that, you and Wendy will have to work it out. I'm only concerned with what happened between you and Julian Walker."

"I warned him to stay away from my wife, and he stormed off in a rage. That was the end of it."

"Where did he go when he left you?"

"The kitchen, I presume. I didn't follow him. I was too busy looking around to see who might have heard us. Fortunately, Wendy wasn't around at that point."

Tess frowned. "Evidently he went to the green room—that's where he was killed."

He looked startled. "How do you know that?"

"The police found Julian's blood in the green room. He was killed there, then moved to the pantry."

He was gripping the edge of the desk again, his knuckles white. "Why would he be moved?"

"So the body wouldn't be found as quickly, I assume," Tess mused, working it out in her mind as she spoke. "The murderer must have thought the kitchen had been vacated by then and didn't expect anybody to go into the pantry until the next day. It was pure bad luck that my cook looked in there when she was searching for her apron."

He pushed to his feet, bracing himself with his hands flat on the desk, and looked down at her. "Are you going to the police with this? I have to know, Tess."

For the first time, Tess felt uneasy, and she was very aware of being alone with him in the office. If Johnny was a murderer, would he kill her, too, to shut her up? She got quickly to her feet and backed toward the door. "If you don't go to the police, I'll have to."

She opened the office door, prepared to bolt through the pro shop if he threatened her.

"I did not kill Julian." Johnny's voice was filled with anguish now. "Why are you doing this to me, Tess?"

"The police have questioned my cook twice now. She's retained a lawyer, even though nobody who knows her believes for a second that she's the murderer. For one thing, she could not have moved the body by herself."

"So you think I could have?"

"You're certainly younger and stronger than Gertie."

"I see what's happening here. You want Gertie Bogart off the hook, so I'm to be the scapegoat." As he spoke, he came around the desk, his hands extended in a gesture of supplication.

"Stay away from me, Johnny!"

His hands dropped to his sides. "I wouldn't hurt you, Tess. You know me, for God's sake."

She had thought so—until the last few days when she'd begun to suspect he was a murderer. Tess hurried from the office and across the pro shop, expecting any moment to feel his hand on her shoulder.

"Tess!"

She didn't look back as she pushed through the pro shop's glass door and into the hallway, colliding with the night security guard.

"Oops," he said, steadying her.

"Sorry, Mr. Blade," Tess said breathlessly. "I didn't see you."

"You all right?"

She nodded, and he looked past her into the shop.

"The pro still in his office?"

"Yes, but I think he's about ready to leave. I wonder, would you mind walking me back to my car?"

"Be glad to. We're all a little edgy these days, after the chef was killed here."

"Were you around that night?"

"Oh, yes. I'm always here when something's going on at night, but mostly I patrol the grounds. We've had a problem with kids trying to steal the golf carts. The way it turned out, I should've been inside that night."

"You couldn't have known that, Mr. Blade," Tess said. "You shouldn't feel guilty."

"Thanks for saying that—Miss Darcy, isn't it?"

"That's right—but only for a few more days."

"I know. You're marrying Luke Fredrik pretty soon now." He placed a hand on her elbow as they walked down the hall together. "Fine young man, Mr. Fredrik."

"He is, yes." They left the building and walked through the warm, still night to Tess's car. Tess got out her keys. "Thanks for the escort, Mr. Blade."

"Any time, ma'am, any time."

He walked back toward the building as she got in and quickly locked the car doors. Her heart was still beating too fast. For a moment there, when Johnny had come around his desk, she'd truly feared for her safety.

Johnny Linzy's demeanor and strained appearance indicated he was under extreme stress. Before tonight, Tess might have believed it was merely worry over his wife finding out about his affair with Raylene. Which would be serious enough, according to Johnny, but now Tess suspected his worry was over something far more serious.

He was acting like a man with more to hide than an extramarital affair, almost like a man in fear for his very life.

Closing her eyes for a moment, she pictured the scene as it might have occurred the night of the barbecue. Walker confronts Johnny, then storms off. Johnny follows Julian back into the club, perhaps trying to reason with him in the green room. Then, when Julian won't listen, Johnny snatches the butcher knife from the pantry, stabs him, and carries the body to the pantry.

Carrying the body would certainly have left blood on Johnny's clothes, but Tess now knew how he could have dealt with that. The night of the barbecue, Johnny had been wearing shorts and one of those knit shirts with the club's logo on the pocket. The pro shop was but a few steps from the green room, in the opposite direction from the pantry. Johnny could easily have gone there and changed to clean shorts and a shirt like the ones he'd been wearing all evening. He'd have locked his bloody clothes in a desk drawer or some other safe place until he could retrieve and destroy them.

It all made perfect sense.

Chapter 21

Sitting in her darkened car, Tess heard the far-off call of an owl. The long, lonesome call matched Tess's mood perfectly. Now that she knew the truth about Johnny and Raylene, she had to go to the police and it would all come out into the open. She had thought she'd feel only relief to be able to give Chief Butts a murder suspect with a strong motive. If it didn't get Gertie off the suspect list completely, it should certainly move her out of the number one slot. Yet, her feelings were decidedly mixed. Not that she wasn't virtually convinced that Johnny was the killer. It wasn't even that she had a lot of sympathy for him. The problem was Johnny's family. Tess's heart went out to Wendy and her son. Would she stand by her husband through a trial? Or would she take the boy away, never to see his father again?

Tess had always liked Johnny, but tonight in his office, his obvious desperation had scared her, and she'd felt rescued when she ran into the security guard. However, to be perfectly honest, she knew Johnny had been right; she was looking for a substitute suspect to give to Chief Butts. Was she using Johnny as a scapegoat, as he'd said?

No, she wouldn't let herself believe that. Certainly

Johnny had been desperate to keep Julian quiet the night of
the barbecue, just as he'd seemed desperate to keep Tess
quiet tonight. Furthermore, he was young and strong, even
though Julian had probably outweighed him by twenty
pounds. As Chief Butts had pointed out, people sometimes
exhibit superhuman strength in a crisis. It was certainly
more plausible that Johnny could have carried Julian's
body from the green room to the pantry than that Gertie
could have done it. And clean clothes exactly like the ones
he'd been wearing all evening were ready at hand. Surely
Chief Butts would realize that Johnny Linzy had had the
means, motive, and opportunity to kill the chef.

So why wasn't she elated?

Tess took out her cell phone and dialed Butts's home
phone. Getting no answer, she dialed the police station and
was told the chief was attending a Kiwanis banquet that
evening at the Hilltop Hotel. She identified herself and left
a message for Butts saying that she had some information
for him and asking him to call her the next day.

As she tucked the phone back in her purse, she noticed
the figure of a man walking slowly away from the building
along the path that circled the golf course and eventually
led to the entrance to the housing addition that overlooked
the course. Johnny Linzy was going home to his wife and
son, perhaps for the last time.

Not wanting to call attention to herself, Tess waited until
he was well out of sight along the path before she started
the engine and drove away.

Still trying to sort through the bewildering mix of feelings in her head, she braked at the crossroad at the corner
of the country club property. She looked left toward the
Linzy's housing addition, but she didn't see Johnny. The
road in that direction curved quickly and, if he'd come this
far, he was beyond the curve only a couple of blocks from
his house.

Tess was about to turn right toward town when she heard

a loud screeching of brakes and then the sound of a car accelerating. From the sound of the speeding car, it was moving away from her location. The noise had come from her left, and it had sounded as though the car had hit something, or almost. She turned left and followed the curving road toward the residential addition.

There was something in the road, just this side of the stone and wrought-iron entrance to the addition. Tess pulled over and jumped out of her car. Only then did she notice the woman huddled against one of the stone pillars, staring at the body in the road as though she were frozen there, with both hands covering the lower half of her face.

"What happened?" Tess called to her as she ran forward and bent over the body. It was Johnny Linzy. Tess pressed her fingers under his jaw for a pulse. The beat was steady. "Call an ambulance!"

The woman didn't move and Tess realized she could be going into shock. She ran to her. "We have to call an ambulance. Do you live around here?"

The woman pointed toward the first house the other side of the entrance. "There."

"Did you see what happened?"

"He ran over him, then drove away."

"Who?"

She shook her head. "It was too dark to see. I was sitting in my front porch swing, having a Coke. Just sitting there. I didn't even see him, until that car came around the corner and the headlights shone on him. The next thing I knew, the car had run over him and then drove away. And I came out here." She peered into the darkness. "It's Johnny Linzy, isn't it?"

"Yes. Do you think you could go call the ambulance now? We shouldn't try to move him. I'm going to stay with him and make sure nobody else runs over him. It's important that we get him to a hospital immediately." It had finally occurred to Tess that she could go back to her car and use her cell phone. But she thought this woman needed something to do to get her moving away from the scene of the accident.

The woman seemed to be trying to pull herself together. "I can't believe this happened in our nice, quiet neighborhood."

"The police," Tess prompted.

"All right," she said and finally moved a few steps, then hurried toward her house. "I guess I should call his wife, too," she muttered as she went.

Tess turned back to Johnny and knelt beside him. "Johnny, can you hear me?" There was no response, but his pulse still beat evenly. She pressed her palm against his forehead, pushing back thick hair. Was she responsible for this? Had her meeting with Johnny upset him so much that he hadn't been paying attention, hadn't heard the car coming?

"Hang on, Johnny," she said urgently. "The ambulance will be here any minute."

Kneeling beside Johnny, she scanned the shadows surrounding the road. Beyond the stone and wrought-iron entrance to Johnny's neighborhood, a few yard lights provided dim illumination. But she saw no one. Evidently the woman in her porch swing was the only one who'd heard the car. Air-conditioning had blanketed the sound for other close neighbors.

She checked Johnny's pulse again and said encouraging things, in case he could hear her. "You're going to make it, Johnny. Just hold on until we can get you to a doctor."

It must have been only minutes, though it seemed like an hour, before she heard the siren. As it came nearer, it sounded loud enough to wake the dead. The ambulance pulled up beside Tess and Johnny, and the driver cut the siren. The silence following the shrieking noise seemed heavily ominous. Just then Wendy Linzy came running through the entrance gates.

"What happened?" Wendy cried. "Where's Johnny?"

The attendants had already jumped out of the ambulance and were checking Johnny for vital signs. "Stand back, ma'am."

Wendy pushed between the attendants and fell to her knees. "Oh, my God! Johnny!"

"He can't hear you, ma'am. He's unconscious," said one of the men.

Another attendant ran up with a litter.

The woman who had made the call had come back out and stood a few feet away. Tess took Wendy's arm and urged her to her feet. "Let them move him to the ambulance, Wendy."

Two of the attendants lifted Johnny to the litter and rushed to the ambulance. Wendy ran after them. "I'm going with him."

Tess heard one of the attendants say, "You can follow us, ma'am."

"That's my husband!" Wendy cried shrilly. "Get out of my way! I'm getting in that ambulance."

The attendant hesitated, studying the near-hysterical woman, and stepped back, allowing her to climb into the rear of the ambulance with Johnny.

Tess walked over to ask, "Is anybody with your son, Wendy?"

The interior light was on in the ambulance, and now Tess could see that Wendy Linzy must have grabbed the first clothes she could put her hands on as she ran through her house. Her shorts were stained with what looked like dirt and her shirt was buttoned crooked. Dirty sneakers completed what appeared to be her gardening outfit. She wore no makeup; she must have been ready for bed when she received the call about her husband.

"Wendy?" Tess asked again.

"A neighbor's with him," Wendy said.

One of the attendants followed Tess as she walked away from the ambulance. "Did anybody see what happened?"

Tess indicated the woman standing a few feet away. "She's the one who called you."

"She told the dispatcher it was a hit-and-run," the attendant said, "so the police will want to talk to her. We notified them as soon as the call came in."

"I'll tell her," Tess said, "and wait here with her."

Tess relayed the message and introduced herself. The woman said, "I'm Liz Turnipseed. Yes, you heard right. It's a Choctaw Indian name. My husband's one-eighth."

"Thanks for making the call, Liz."

They walked back to Liz Turnipseed's house and sat in the swing. "That poor woman," Liz said. "What a terrible thing to find your husband like that."

"I'd just seen Johnny at the country club," Tess said. "I was going home when I heard the car. Could you tell what kind it was?"

Liz shook her head. "I'm hopeless with cars. They all look alike to me. It looked dark, but then there was very little light, except for the car's headlights."

"I heard the driver hit the brakes. Was that when he'd hit Johnny?"

"No—before. He skidded a little, but he almost came to a stop. I recognized Johnny when the headlights shone on him. He just stood there, like he was paralyzed. The car couldn't have been more than eight or ten feet from him."

"Are you saying the driver slowed down and *then* ran over Johnny?"

"Yes. After a moment, Johnny must've realized the car had stopped and he was OK, then he started to walk over to the edge of the road. That's when the driver hit the accelerator and ran right over him. I swear it looked like he did it on purpose. And he didn't even slow down. He sped through the neighborhood—he must've been going sixty. Thank goodness it's too late for any of the neighborhood kids to be out playing."

"Is it possible he lives here, in this neighborhood?"

"I don't think so. I kept hearing the sound of the car

engine get dimmer and dimmer until I couldn't hear it anymore. He definitely left the neighborhood. There are three
other exits besides the main entrance."

Seemingly exhausted by the spate of words, the woman
slumped back in the swing and remained quiet for several
moments. Then, "I couldn't believe my eyes. Maybe the
driver's foot accidentally slipped off the brake and hit the
accelerator," she mused hopefully. "Do you think that's
what happened?"

"I don't know."

"If it was an accident, when he realized what he'd done,
he could've panicked and run away."

"It's possible," Tess said. The driver's heart must've
been pounding furiously as he realized how close he'd
come to hitting Johnny. That would send anybody's anxiety through the roof. She could imagine him accidentally
hitting the accelerator at such a moment.

So why was her gut instinct telling her that Johnny
Linzy had been deliberately run down?

Chapter 22

A morning shower had cooled the temperature a few degrees, enough so that Tess did not immediately begin to perspire as she stepped out of her car. There was even a little breeze whispering through the trees scattered over the wide, rolling grounds, moving the leaves so that it sounded like rain falling softly.

"Think this cool spell will last?" asked Cinny as she walked with Tess toward the hospital.

Cinny had called first thing that morning, having heard about what happened to Johnny Linzy. She wanted to pay a visit to the hospital and asked Tess to go with her. As Tess had planned to come anyway, she said she'd drive by for Cinny. On the trip to the hospital, she'd told Cinny that she'd been leaving the country club when Johnny Linzy was run down and related what little she knew about the incident.

"No," Tess said now, "I don't think this will last. We still have July and August to get through."

"At least you're leaving town for a while. I hope Luke's chosen someplace cool for your honeymoon. Do you really not know where you're going?"

"Not for sure. But I once mentioned that I'd love to take an Alaskan cruise. That may be what he's arranged."

166

"Sounds lovely. Should be a nice time to see Alaska," Cinny said. "By the way, I ordered flowers for Johnny and put both our names on the card. They'll be delivered to the hospital today."

"Good. I'll pay you later."

Tess felt Cinny's eyes on her as she passed through the automatic doors and entered the clean, tiled, air-conditioned reception area. "What were you doing at the country club last night?"

"Checking a few things for the reception," Tess said vaguely.

"Tess?" Cinny said sharply.

Tess glanced at her cousin. "What?"

"Why do I get the feeling you're holding back? Have you told me everything you know about Johnny's accident?"

"If it was an accident," Tess said. "Liz Turnipseed thinks it was deliberate. And, yes, I've told you all I know about it."

"It doesn't make any sense," Cinny said. "Who'd want to run over a golf pro? A disgruntled golfer? Somebody whose application for membership in the club was turned down? It's crazy."

Tess was not ready to tell Cinny the real reason she'd gone to the club last night. She certainly wasn't going to mention Johnny and Raylene's affair or the resulting pregnancy. In view of Johnny's condition, it seemed prudent to tell no one except Chief Butts until they knew if Johnny would live or die.

Inquiring at the desk, they were given Johnny's room number. When they stepped off the elevator into the third floor waiting room, Officer Andy Neill lounged on a green vinyl couch.

"Hi, Andy," Tess greeted him. "What're you doing here?"

"Waiting for the chief," Neill said. "He's talking to Mrs. Linzy."

Andy had been the officer on call last night; he'd come

to Liz Turnipseed's house to take her statement. Tess had stayed with Liz until Neill was gone, leaving only when Liz assured her she'd be fine, that her husband was working late but should be home any minute.

"Tess," Andy said, "I don't guess Mrs. Turnipseed remembered anything else about that hit-and-run vehicle last night after I talked to her."

"No," Tess said. "I honestly think she told you everything she saw."

"She wasn't much help. Didn't know what kind of car it was, not even the color. Couldn't even tell if the driver was a man or a woman."

"I know," Tess said unhappily.

At that moment, Chief Butts walked into the waiting room from the hallway leading to the patient rooms. Upon spotting Tess, he said, "I was going to call you. Neill says you phoned the station last night, asking for me."

Tess glanced at Cinny and Neill. "Could we go down the hall a ways, Chief?" she asked, and without waiting for his reply, started in that direction.

Butts followed her. "Some coincidence," he said, "you being there last night when Linzy got run over."

"That's what I wanted to talk to you about. I had a meeting with Johnny at the club shortly before that. He walked home and I was going home, too, when I heard screeching brakes and then a car speeding away. I went to investigate and found Johnny lying in the street. Liz Turnipseed had just arrived on the scene, too, and she went back to her house and called for an ambulance."

"Neill talked to her. Typical eyewitness account. Not much help."

"She seemed pretty sure it was no accident."

He nodded. "If you can believe a hysterical woman."

"She wasn't hysterical, Chief. She was shocked, but she got hold of herself and phoned for the ambulance."

"Why were you meeting with Linzy? He doesn't give golf lessons at night, does he?"

"He's the father of Raylene Walker's child."

That got Butts's attention. "You sure?'

"Yes. I went there to tell him I knew and that I'd go to the police with the information if he didn't."

"He admitted it?"

"As much as," Tess told him. "The night of the murder, Julian Walker learned Raylene was pregnant and knew it couldn't be his child. He accused Johnny and told him he should be prepared to support the child for the next eighteen years. Then he threatened to go to Wendy. Johnny was desperate to stop him."

"You're not telling me Johnny confessed to the murder."

"No, he denied it. But I left the club convinced Johnny Linzy murdered Julian Walker. I even figured out why his clothes didn't have any blood on them later that night."

Butts's bushy eyebrows rose another fraction of an inch. "Care to let me in on it?"

"Ever since we found Julian's blood on the blind in the green room, I've been trying to figure out how the murderer kept from getting blood on his clothes. Earlier on the night of the murder, Johnny was wearing shorts and a shirt from the pro shop. All he had to do was change into an identical outfit in his office and hide the bloody clothes until he could dispose of them later. He was wandering around the club all evening, from the patio to the green room to his office and who knows where else. It would have been easy for him to get to his office and change clothes with nobody being the wiser."

"*If* he killed Walker."

"He's surely a better suspect than Gertie Bogart."

"I'll admit he had a motive. But if he killed Walker, and if that hit-and-run last night really was deliberate, then who was in that car? And why was he trying to kill Linzy?"

That very thing had been nagging at Tess ever since the night before. Further, was the hit-and-run a spur-of-the-moment decision, or had the driver known Johnny would be walking from the club to his house at that particular time? Who, besides Johnny's wife, could have known that?

"I don't have the answers, Chief," Tess said.

"Maybe Linzy will wake up and tell us," Butts said with no real conviction in his voice.

"He's still unconscious?"

"In a coma. The nurse says there's no way of telling when, or if, he will come out of it."

"How's his wife doing?"

"She looked to me like somebody who'd been run over by a train. Right before I left, the nurse convinced her to go down to the cafeteria for something to eat."

"Maybe I can get her to go home for a rest. I'll tell her I'll stay with Johnny."

A few minutes later Tess was gazing at Johnny Linzy's silent form with the tube that was delivering life-sustaining liquid from a bottle taped to his arm. His right leg was in a cast. A sick feeling twisted her stomach. What if Johnny never regained consciousness? What if the police never found that hit-and-run driver? What if they never knew for sure who had killed Julian Walker?

Standing beside Tess, Cinny whispered, "He looks dead."

"Shh," Tess cautioned. "For all we know, he can hear what's going on around him, even in a coma."

Johnny's face was sun-tanned from all the hours he spent on the course, but something about it now looked unnatural. Perhaps it was the utter lack of expression, the deathlike stillness.

"We can't do anything here," Cinny muttered.

Tess nodded, but as she turned, from the corner of her eye she thought she saw Johnny's eyelids flutter. She turned back. "Johnny?" There was no response. She followed Cinny quietly from the room. When they emerged, they saw Wendy, carrying a Styrofoam cup, coming toward them. She still wore the same dirt-stained clothes she'd had on last night. Strain lined her face and made her look old. If they couldn't do anything for Johnny, maybe they could assist Wendy.

"Have you had breakfast?" Tess asked as Wendy reached them.

"A Danish," Wendy said. "I didn't want to be gone too long." She crept to the door of Johnny's room and looked in. "He hasn't moved since I left. He hasn't moved since they put him in that bed last night." Her voice broke and she swallowed tears. "His leg was broken in two places, but no other broken bones. He must have banged his head, though, when the car ran over his leg."

"If you'd like to go home and get a shower, change clothes," Tess said, "we could stay with him."

"No." She took a swallow of coffee from the Styrofoam cup and made a face. "Nasty stuff, but I need the caffeine."

"You need to get some rest," Cinny said.

"I slept for a couple of hours in a chair in Johnny's room. I called my neighbor this morning and she said I shouldn't worry about Marcus. He can stay with her until my father gets here tomorrow. I can't leave Johnny like that." Tears sprang to her eyes. "The—the doctor says he could regain consciousness at any time."

Or never, Tess thought. But that was a possibility Wendy wasn't ready to consider just yet.

"I tried to get him not to go back to the club last night," Wendy said. "If only he'd listened to me . . ."

"Why *did* he go back?" Tess asked.

"He had a meeting. And then he decided to walk. He said he needed the time to think."

"Do you know what kind of meeting it was, or with whom?"

Wendy shook her head. "He didn't say. I guess I didn't really ask. It didn't seem important at the time." She took another swallow of coffee, grimaced again, then walked a few feet to a waste container and dropped the half-full cup in. Turning back, she said, "This morning Chief Butts told me that Liz Turnipseed is saying the car ran Johnny down deliberately." She appeared suddenly lost and she searched Tess's face as if she were looking for an explanation there.

"Was Johnny in some kind of trouble, Wendy?" Tess asked.

"Trouble?"

"I mean," Tess amended, "if this was no accident, there has to be a reason. Was he having problems with somebody at the club?"

Cinny was studying Tess with interest. "Why somebody at the club?" she asked.

"Because that's where he went to meet whoever it was. And Johnny was hit walking home from there."

Wendy frowned. "I don't know. He did mention once that he could lose his job."

"He's very well-liked," Tess said. "Why would he think he might lose his job?" But immediately it occurred to her why. If the affair with Raylene Walker came out, he could well be asked to resign.

"He wouldn't say," Wendy replied. "But he's been worried about something for quite a while. He wouldn't talk about it. I—I thought it was money. Most of the arguments we've had in our marriage have been over money. He thinks I'm a spendthrift. And I think he's too touchy on the subject of my father and his money. Daddy wants to make our life easier, and Johnny resents it." She shrugged helplessly. "I've never understood his attitude."

Tess could easily understand. A man whose father-in-law funneled money to his daughter over her husband's objections had to feel less than adequate, even insulted, and helpless to do anything about it.

"I guess it's a man thing," Wendy added, going back to the door to look in at her husband.

"Isn't there something we can do for you?" Tess asked.

Wendy shook her head. "I can't think of anything, but

it's thoughtful of you to ask. People have been very kind. Jed Baskin was here earlier. And Paula Overton called this morning. So did the chairman of the governing board, Wayne Trammell. Everybody wants to help, but there's nothing they can do."

"Maybe you'll think of something later," Tess said. "I'll check back with you this afternoon."

"You're very kind." She looked in at her husband. "The doctor said I should keep talking to him. I guess they don't know a lot about coma—how much patients can hear or know while they're in one. I'm going to read the newspaper to him later."

"We'll be going then," Tess said.

Wendy murmured her thanks and slipped back into the room to take up a vigil beside her husband's bed.

As they left the hospital, Cinny asked, "What was your little confab with Chief Butts about?"

"I just wanted to let him know how I came to be on the scene right after Johnny was hit. I couldn't really give him any new information about the hit-and-run."

"That Turnipseed woman is sure it was no accident?"

"That's how she saw it," Tess said. They had reached her car. They got in and she started the motor and turned up the air-conditioning.

"It's too weird," Cinny mused. "Walker is murdered at the club, and then Johnny Linzy is hit walking away from there."

"I'd sure like to know who Johnny had that meeting with last night."

"Surely somebody out there will know."

"I didn't see anybody but the security guard."

"Maybe he knows who Johnny met with."

"I didn't think to ask him last night," Tess said. Her mind had been on getting safely back to her car and away from Johnny. "I'll try to catch Mr. Blade today."

The first thing Tess did when she got home was to call

the security guard's office at the club. She got the answering machine and asked Blade to call her back. Which he did shortly thereafter.

"Mr. Blade, have you heard about Johnny Linzy's accident?"

"Yes, ma'am. Terrible thing. Terrible."

"Johnny had a meeting with somebody in his office last night, before I got there. Do you know who it was?"

"No."

"You didn't see anybody around his office about seven or so?"

"No, ma'am. The place was as silent as a tomb, until you came out of the pro shop."

Tess sighed. "Thanks, anyway, Mr. Blade."

That night, Raylene Walker watched the ten o'clock news before going to bed. Julian's body had been released and cremated that day. She'd asked the funeral home to store the urn for her until she could pick it up. She hadn't yet decided what to do with it. She certainly didn't want to keep Julian's ashes in the house.

Now she looked with disinterest at the lead news story, the death of a former mayor of Springfield, where the newscast originated, and at the weather forecast—hot and dry, more of what they'd been having the last week.

Just before sign-off, there was a snippet about Johnny Linzy's hit-and-run. Raylene had already heard about it in town, and she was hungry for more information. She couldn't ask Wendy, and inquiring at the club didn't seem like the best idea, either. So she listened intently to every word the newscaster said.

Johnny was identified as the golf pro at the Victoria Springs Country Club. The driver of the car had still not been identified, and the police were asking for any information the public might have. The story ended with the statement that Linzy remained in a coma at Victoria Springs Hospital.

Raylene turned off the set, disappointed that the story had contained no new information. She went to the kitchen and looked out at the backyard. As unsatisfactory as her marriage had been, living alone was lonelier than she had ever imagined it would be. She had made very few friends in Victoria Springs, and none with whom she felt close enough to share her deepest thoughts and feelings.

She placed her hand on the barely detectable bulge of her stomach. At least, in six months she would no longer be alone. By then, perhaps the police would have charged somebody with Julian's murder, and she could claim the insurance money. She wanted desperately to know how the investigation was progressing. Had Chief Butts zeroed in on a prime suspect? She didn't dare contact him, for fear of calling more attention to herself. He'd questioned her three times, the last only yesterday. Each time he contacted her to ask for another interview, she got a knot the size of a fist in her stomach. Was this the time he was coming to arrest her? Her nerves were frazzled almost constantly now, and she had trouble sleeping. It couldn't be good for the baby.

She wanted this baby so much—wanted someone to love and care for. But sometimes she cried when she thought that this child would never know its father. She realized now that Johnny had never really loved her. She had been but a brief distraction from his everyday life. But she had loved him. Maybe because she was disillusioned with her marriage and so desperately needed somebody to love. On her side, at least, this baby had been created out of more than mere lust.

She would protect her child with her life. She had always heard about the fierceness of maternal feelings, but she had never expected to feel them so strongly before she even held the baby in her arms.

He, or she, would never know that his real father didn't want him, that he was married to someone else and wanted her to abort the fetus. If Julian had lived and gone through with the divorce, how would she have provided for this child? She didn't know and was grateful she wouldn't have to find out. She *would* get the insurance money eventually, and the mortgage insurance would provide her and the baby with a debt-free place to live. Meanwhile, she could get by if she watched every penny.

Another thing she would give the baby was a loving father. Not Johnny, of course. She had come to realize that exposing him as her child's father would serve no useful purpose. Julian would be the father. He would become a devoted husband and a man who was looking forward to being a doting parent in the later years of his life. She would make up stories for the baby about how Julian talked of taking the family on camping trips and the big Disney World vacation he was planning even before the child was born. Her baby would never know it was all a pack of lies.

For a few minutes, she practiced the breathing exercises that brought her serenity for a while. Then she went to the den and opened the scrapbook she had started yesterday. It would provide her child with all he needed to know about the man he would believe was his father.

Chapter 23

A few minutes after her conversation with the security guard, Tess's father tapped on her door.

"What's up, Dad?"

He gave her a bear hug. "Just wanted to visit with my elder daughter. We've had very little time alone since I got here."

"Come on in the kitchen and I'll make us some tea," Tess invited, leading the way.

"I really like what you've done to this place," Frank said, settling into one of the chairs at the kitchen table. "Plenty of room for you and Luke and a couple of kids."

She smiled at him as she took two cups from the cupboard. "We do want kids, Dad, but not for a few years yet."

"Wise decision."

She made the tea and brought it and a plate of butter cookies to the table. "You must be having fun, spending time with your old college buddies."

He grinned. "Sure am. You know how it is with old friends. Even when you see them rarely, you can pick up right where you left off. No matter how important they get, you knew them when they pulled some stupid tricks—like the time Oliver tried to slip into the girls' dorm and fell off the second-story roof."

Tess laughed. "Did he break anything?"

"No, but he was banged up for a week." His expression turned thoughtful. "Good old Oliver. I hope that land deal comes through for him. He's really counting on that million to set up a retirement trust." He frowned. "I know Wayne's pushing for it with the board. Personally, I'm afraid Wayne's letting their friendship affect his opinion. According to a guy I met on the golf course, the architect says there's another site that would serve about as well and it's less expensive."

"I'm sure the board will make the right decision," Tess said.

"Yeah, and it's none of my business. Wayne has always been loyal to his friends, and right now, he doesn't need any hassle, with all he has on his mind—" He broke off to bite into a butter cookie.

"All he has on his mind?' Tess prompted.

Frank made a face. "This is between you and me, honey. But Wayne's planning to divorce Esther."

"Is Esther aware of this?"

He shook his head. "Oliver says Wayne's been funneling money to an offshore account for quite a while."

"Money he doesn't want Esther to know about?"

"Right. He's afraid she'll take him to the cleaner's in the divorce, so he wants to hide as much money as possible. After the divorce, he plans to start over somewhere else. Apparently the last year or so he's been spending as little time at home as possible. He keeps clothes and toiletries in his locker at the club. Oliver says he's even spent a few nights on the couch in the locker room."

"I'm sorry to hear it," Tess said. "Wayne and Esther have been married for a long time."

"Yeah, and evidently they haven't communicated about anything important for years. Wayne says now that he should have left her long ago, but he stayed until their children were out of the house. Since then, I gather he's been hanging on while he builds his nest egg." He reached across the table to pat Tess's hand. "Hey, this is depressing. Let's talk about something else."

He stayed for almost an hour, until Curt came looking for him. Zelda wanted to pick up a few things in town. "Want to come with us?" Frank asked Tess. She declined, saying she had lists to make. If she didn't write down everything she still needed to do before the wedding, she'd forget something important.

But when she'd closed the door behind them, she couldn't get her mind on lists. Something was nagging at the back of her mind. Something she and her father had talked about? She returned to the kitchen to wash and dry the dirty cups and tried to pin down what it was. Did it have to do with Wayne and Esther and their divorce? No, she didn't think so. In her mind, she replayed the conversation with her father. It took a while, but she finally pulled up what was bothering her.

She went to her office to phone her Aunt Dahlia. "Oh, hi, Tess. Cinny tells me Johnny Linzy is still in a coma. What a shame."

"Yes, it is," Tess agreed.

"Are you sure it was no accident?" Why did everybody expect her to know the answer to that?

"I'm not sure of anything, Aunt Dahlia. All I know is that the woman who saw the car hit Johnny says it appeared deliberate to her. Chief Butts is looking into it. I wanted to talk to you about something else."

"What, dear?"

"Have you heard Uncle Maurice say how much money the new golf course site is going to cost?"

"Let me think now," Dahlia mused. "Sometimes when Maurice starts talking money, my eyes glaze over. I do remember that it sounded like a lot to me. I believe the asking price for one piece of land is something like a million and a half."

"Is that the one Oliver Stedman owns?"

"No, he wants more for that piece. Of course, it does

front the road, while the other one doesn't. I believe he's asking a little over two million. Maurice thinks they can negotiate the price down to two, though." This was what had been nagging at Tess. She had heard a price of two million tossed around in conversations at the club.

"Wow, that's a lot of money—in either case. Do you know which site they're going to buy?"

"They're supposed to take a vote soon. Johnny Linzy insists that Stedman's land is much the better, and Wayne Trammell is backing him."

"With Johnny in a coma, will that change?"

"I doubt it. In fact, I wouldn't be surprised if a couple of the board members who've been holding out decide to go along with Wayne out of sympathy for Johnny. The others have said all along that Johnny's in a better position than anybody else to know which site is more suitable. Why are you interested in this, Tess?"

"Something Dad said made me curious. It's not important, Aunt Dahlia. I'll talk to you later."

She hung up thinking that her father must have misunderstood Oliver Stedman. The price of his land was two million, not the one million her father had mentioned.

Having sorted that out, Tess went to her office and made two lists—one, of the things she needed to do the next day, the other, of things that must be done in the days following that. Just one week now until her wedding day. She chewed the end of her ballpoint pen reflectively. One week, and she still hadn't proved Gertie's innocence beyond a doubt to Chief Butts.

Later, Luke came by to take her to dinner, after which he asked if she'd mind going to the hospital with him to check on Johnny Linzy. "As far as I know," Luke said, "he's still in a coma, but I want to pay my respects to Wendy."

Wendy wasn't in Johnny's room when they arrived. "I hope she's gone home to get some rest," Tess murmured, looking down at Johnny's still form. "I tried to get her to go earlier, but she wouldn't."

A nurse came in, padding softly on rubber soles, and checked Johnny's vital signs. "How's he doing?" Luke asked.

"About the same," said the nurse.

"At least he doesn't seem to be in any pain," Luke said.

The nurse nodded solemnly. "Coma may be the body's way of recuperating until it's ready to start feeling again."

"So you do think he'll come out of it," Tess said.

"I didn't say that. I've known of people remaining in a comatose state for years. Don't stay too long now." She padded out of the room.

"Cheerful woman," Luke said grimly.

Johnny's arms lay at his sides on top of the sheet, which was pulled up to his waist. The bulge of his leg cast was clearly visible beneath the covering. Tess touched his wrist. His skin felt cool. "Nurses don't know everything," she said. "He'll come out of it. Won't you, Johnny?"

Luke put an arm around her shoulders. "Think he can hear you?"

"Maybe." As Tess watched Johnny, his right eyelid fluttered, just as it had before when she was there. She bent over him. "Johnny, you can hear me, can't you?"

Footsteps sounded on the polished floor outside and Wendy hurried into the room, carrying a sandwich and iced drink. "Back again, Tess?"

"Luke wanted to come by," Tess said.

"Everybody is being so kind." She looked at the paper-wrapped sandwich in her hand and sighed. "Hospital food." She had, however, been home at some point, for she'd exchanged her dirt-stained shorts and shirt for a green-and-white-checked pantsuit. She laid the sandwich on the bedside table. "Thank you for the flowers, Tess," she said, gesturing toward three vases lined up on the wide window ledge. "Yours and Cinny's is the azalea. Wayne

Trammell brought the roses from the board, and the mixed bouquet is from the club employees."

"I could sit with him tonight," Tess suggested, "if you'd like to go home for a few hours."

"I wouldn't be able to sleep," Wendy said, patting Johnny's arm gently. She bent over him and brushed a speck from his cheek.

"Did you see that?" Tess asked.

Wendy peered at her husband. "What?"

"I thought I saw his eyelid move," Tess said urgently. "Didn't you see it?"

Wendy shook her head. "No. You imagined it, Tess."

"Keep looking," Tess said. "There, he did it again."

Suddenly Johnny's nose twitched and he sneezed and his eyes flew open. "Sorry, Wendy," he said. "I couldn't help it."

"Oh, Johnny . . ." Wendy's gaze darted to Tess and Luke. "Tess, Luke, you must keep this quiet."

Tess was trying to understand what was going on. "He's not in a coma. Has he ever been?"

"Only for a few hours," Wendy said. "He's afraid whoever tried to kill him will try again if word gets out that he's conscious. Even his doctor doesn't know. It's getting harder and harder to pretend when the doctor and nurses come in."

"Johnny," Luke said, "do you know who tried to run you down?"

"Maybe," he muttered.

"Who?" Tess asked urgently.

"He won't even tell me," Wendy said.

"I don't know for sure. And I can't prove my suspicions," Johnny told them. "I don't want to say anything till I'm out of here. You two have to promise to keep my secret."

He grimaced and Wendy asked, "Are you in pain, sweetheart?"

"It's not so bad."

"We'll let you rest," Tess said.

Wendy followed Tess and Luke into the hall. "I'm so worried about him," she confided. "I've tried to get him to talk to Chief Butts, but he won't. So I stay with him almost all the time so I can warn him when somebody's coming. He's so worried and I know that's not good for him."

"He really thinks somebody tried to kill him and will try again?" Tess asked.

Wendy nodded, frowning. "He's sure of it, but he's not telling me everything. When he first started coming out of the coma, he kept saying he didn't want the money. But he won't tell me what money he's talking about." Suddenly, Wendy burst into tears. Tess led her to a bench a few feet down the hall. Wendy dried her eyes with the tail of her shirt. "I asked him if he's worried about taking my father's money." Lacing her fingers together, she pressed her hands against her chest, almost as if she were praying. "He doesn't want to talk about it. I never meant . . . oh, Tess, I never realized how strongly he felt about that. I guess I didn't want to know. I've told him I'll never take another dime from my father without his permission. But it didn't seem to ease his worry."

Luke walked slowly up to the bench where they sat. "He can't keep pretending to be unconscious indefinitely," he said. "The doctor is bound to catch on."

"It almost happened earlier today," Wendy said. "We're probably going to have to confide in the doctor soon. Until then you two must keep quiet."

"We will," Tess promised, hoping it was the right decision.

Later that night, Wendy called Iris House as Tess was getting ready for bed. "I wanted to let you know, Tess," she said, "that the doctor came in a while ago and caught

Johnny with his eyes open. I'd fallen asleep and Johnny didn't hear him coming. So the secret is out." She sounded weary beyond words. "Now I'll be afraid to leave his side at all."

Chapter 24

Tess gave her family the encouraging news about Johnny Linzy the next morning at breakfast—all except Madison and Curt, who were sleeping in.

"I wonder if Wayne knows?" Frank asked. "He's been really worried about Linzy."

Oliver consulted his wristwatch. "We can tell him in about forty minutes, Frank. That's when we're due at the club for a round of golf." He buttered a second biscuit. "We should leave pretty soon."

Frank ate the remainder of his scrambled eggs and drained his coffee cup. "Zelda, Ruth, are you sure you don't mind being left on your own again?"

"Since when have you needed to entertain me?" Zelda asked.

Ruth smiled at her husband. "I'm glad to see Oliver enjoying himself. He rarely has time for recreation when we're home."

"I'll be ready in ten minutes," Frank said, pushing back his chair. "Meet you in the foyer, Oliver."

The women lingered in the dining room over coffee until the men left Iris House. "Is there anything I can do to help you today, Tess?" Zelda asked.

Tess shook her head. "No, thanks. My bridal gown should be ready today. I'll pick it up when I'm in town."

"I can do that, Tess," Zelda said.

"I hate to keep sending you on my errands."

"I don't mind, really. In fact, that's why we came two weeks before the wedding—to help you."

"OK. I'll give you the address. You don't need an appointment. Just pick it up when it's convenient."

"Will do."

Tess released a satisfied sigh. "I think I have everything else under control. Has Maddie tried on her maid-of-honor gown since the seamstress delivered it?"

"Oh, yes." Zelda smiled indulgently. "It's a perfect fit, and Maddie looks lovely in it."

"Maddie would look lovely in anything," Ruth observed.

"I have to agree," Zelda told her, "even if she is my daughter. I'm so glad she took after Frank's side of the family instead of mine."

"She looks an awful lot like Aunt Dahlia's pictures, when she was a teenager," Tess said.

"That's what Frank says," Zelda agreed. "Well, I think I'll go up to the suite and read for a couple of hours. Ruth, would you like to go to town for lunch with the kids and me? We can pick up Tess's gown on the way back."

"Sounds good," Ruth said. "We could try that tearoom Tess recommended."

"We'll leave a little before noon, then." Zelda went upstairs, leaving Tess and Ruth Stedman alone at the dining table.

"I thought I'd check out your library this morning, Tess," Ruth said. "I finished the novel I brought with me last night."

"Help yourself," Tess said, but as Ruth prepared to leave the table, she detained her by saying, "From something Dad said, I gather Oliver is planning to retire soon."

"It can't be soon enough for me," Ruth told her. "The man works all the time." A troubled frown creased her brow. "We had a little scare with his heart last year. The doctor told him to slow down, and he did for a while, but he's gotten back in his old rut of working ten and twelve hours a day. Frankly, Tess, the sale of his land here couldn't have come at a better time." She lifted a hand with fingers crossed. "If the sale goes through. And Wayne seems to think it will."

"Two million dollars should make for a comfortable retirement," Tess said.

"Well, of course, Wayne will only get half that, but it will certainly be enough."

"Oh. I assumed the land was paid for."

"It is."

"Then I don't understand . . ."

"The land belongs to the corporation Oliver formed years ago." Ruth dropped her napkin beside her plate and stood.

"So there are partners?"

"Just one. And that's all I know about it. Business bores me." She dropped her napkin beside her plate and stood. "I'll be in the library if anybody needs me, Tess."

For the rest of the day, Tess felt restless.

Was Johnny right? Would the driver of the hit-and-run car try again to kill him? Why? And who was Oliver Stedman's phantom corporate partner?

Late that afternoon, she called the hospital and was put through to Johnny's room. Wendy answered.

"How's he doing?" Tess asked.

"Physically, he's doing well, according to the doctor, but he's very tense. Last night in his sleep, he was still saying he doesn't want the money. I've tried and tried to assure him that I understand, that I won't take any more from my father. I don't know if he believes me or not."

"Are you sure that's the money he's talking about?"

The line was so quiet Tess thought it had gone dead. Then Wendy said, "What other money could it be?"

I don't know, Tess thought, but Johnny's concern about money troubled her.

"My father finally got here," Wendy said. "He's staying at the house with Marcus. Daddy's very good with him, so that's one worry off my mind. Marcus keeps asking about his father. As soon as Johnny is more awake, I'll have Dad bring Marcus for a short visit."

"I'll be at the hospital around noon," Tess said. "You can get something to eat while I sit with Johnny."

Tess stepped into the elevator. Turning around, she saw Raylene Walker running across the hospital foyer toward her.

"Thanks for holding for me," Raylene said breathlessly. She looked fresh and rested in a sleeveless cotton dress. Tess had not noticed before what a dewy complexion Raylene had. Perhaps it was the bloom that fell on pregnant women that she'd heard about. Tess punched the button for Johnny's floor and the doors slid closed.

"Are you here to see Johnny, too?" Raylene asked.

"Yes, I want to give Wendy a break for lunch. She won't leave Johnny alone."

"Ever since one of the club members called to tell me about the accident, I've been stewing over whether or not I should come and see him," Raylene said. "When I called the nurses' station this morning and learned he'd regained consciousness, I knew I had to."

"I'm not sure it's a good idea, Raylene."

"I had to," she said again.

Wendy sat with her arms folded on the bedside table, her cheek resting on her arms, asleep. But her eyes flew open as soon as they walked into the room. She sat up and yawned behind her hand.

"Hi," she said. "Oh, Raylene, you're so sweet to come here with all you've been going through. How are you doing?"

"OK," Raylene told her, gazing at Johnny's sleeping form.

Johnny's hand moved and he mumbled something. Wendy bent over him and caressed his brow. "You've got visitors, sweetheart. Tess is here again, and Raylene's with her."

He opened his eyes and peered into his wife's face. For a moment, he seemed to struggle for words. "Love you," he said.

"I love you, too, darling. Do you feel like saying hello to Tess and Raylene?"

He didn't reply, and his gaze remained fixed on Wendy's face.

"I hear you're going to be fine, Johnny," Raylene said and moved to the side of the bed.

Tess felt very uneasy about Raylene's being there. From the way Wendy had greeted her, it was evident that Wendy knew nothing about the affair, and Tess wondered what had possessed Raylene to come.

"Can I share some good news?" Raylene said.

Wendy turned to smile at her. "We could all use some about now."

"I'm going to have a baby."

Tess was watching Johnny. His gaze darted to his wife, then back to Raylene. His eyes seemed to be pleading.

Wendy didn't notice Johnny's reaction because she had turned to give Raylene an impulsive hug. "I'm so happy for you, Raylene. I guess this isn't the best timing for you but—"

"Actually, it is. It gives me something to look forward to. My only regret is that Julian didn't live to see his child." Her eyes held Johnny's as she said it. "I'm making a scrapbook about Julian for the baby. There are a couple of articles that appeared in the San Francisco paper on the food page, and snapshots from the time he was a child up until his death."

"What a great idea," Tess said.

"I want our baby to know that his father was a good man and would have loved him very much."

Johnny's whole body seemed to relax, and he closed his eyes. Then he sighed and went back to sleep or pretended to.

"I don't want to tire him," Raylene said, "so I'll go now. Wendy, let me know if there's anything I can do for you."

"Thank you for coming, Raylene."

"Wendy," Tess said, "go get something to eat. I'll stay here with Johnny."

"I will. I didn't have breakfast and I'm starving. Right now even the cafeteria food seems appealing."

Wendy left and Tess followed Raylene into the hall to say, "Thank you."

"For what?"

"For saying Julian is the baby's father."

Raylene sighed, "I know you think it's Johnny."

"I will never say that to anybody else."

"Thank you."

"I think Johnny understood your message and was grateful."

"It was something I needed to do," she said simply. "I'm glad if it helps him rest easier."

Chapter 25

That evening, Tess borrowed Gertie's ice cream freezer and made strawberry ice cream for Luke and her family. They gathered at nine on the patio, after the day's heat had dissipated enough to make sitting outside a pleasant experience.

"This is the best homemade ice cream I ever tasted," her father said as he went back to the freezer for a second helping.

"It's Gertie's recipe," Tess said. "I get all my best recipes from Gertie."

"Is Chief Butts still harassing her?" Cinny asked. She had come with her parents, as Cody was out of town on business.

"Not since Cody talked to him," Tess said. "That doesn't mean he's taken her off the suspect list, though. He's like a pit bull when he gets his teeth into something—or somebody."

"It'll turn out all right in the end, Tess," Zelda said. "Even if the chief eventually arrests Gertie, I can't believe she'd be convicted in a court of law."

"It's certainly not unheard of for innocent people to be convicted and imprisoned," Cinny said.

"Aren't you cheerful tonight?" asked Dahlia.

"It's that lawyer she's been keeping company with," Cinny's father teased.

"If they try to arrest Gertie," Curt said indignantly, "maybe we could hide her. We could take her to one of those safe houses you hear about on TV."

"Those are for people in the witness protection program," Maddie said disdainfully. "Or women who are hiding from husbands who beat them."

"We could get our own safe house!" Curt insisted. "Maybe in Paris so she could visit us."

There were several chuckles, and Tess, who was seated beside her brother, reached out to hug him. "Let's keep that one on hold as a last resort, Curt."

"Ah," Maurice sighed. "I'm stuffed."

Frank began gathering up bowls and spoons. Tess followed him to the kitchen. "Dad, could I ask you something?"

"Sure, honey."

"Do you know anything about Oliver's corporation?"

"I don't think he works for a corporation. It's a small business."

"No, I mean the corporation he set up. Ruth says the land the country club is interested in is owned by the corporation."

Her father turned from arranging bowls in the dishwasher. "Really? It's news to me. He probably did it for tax purposes."

"Hmm. Ruth also said he has a partner. I don't guess you'd know who that is."

"No." He closed the dishwasher door and straightened up.

"Don't you think it's odd that Oliver never mentioned the corporation to you?"

He frowned thoughtfully. "Not really, Tess. We don't talk business much when we get together."

"Would you mind asking him who his partner is?"

He looked at her quizzically for a long moment. "I don't

know why you're interested in this, Tess. But if the subject comes up, I'll ask."

Tess did not think the subject would come up, and something about that troubled her.

It was after ten when Tess and Luke were left alone and Luke said, "You're preoccupied, love."

It was true. In her mind, she'd been turning over several thoughts concerning Oliver and his corporation. Now, she'd come up with a possible conclusion that made the hair stand up on the back of her head. Instead of responding to Luke's observation, she said, "Sweetheart, I need to go to the hospital."

They were still on the patio, lounging in the redwood settee with Luke's arm around her and her head on his shoulder. At her words, he lifted her face so that he could see it in the light of a yard lamp. His expression was concerned. "Are you feeling ill, love?"

Tess sat up straight. "No, but I have to talk to Johnny Linzy."

"At this hour?"

"I can't explain it, Luke. It just feels urgent to me."

He ran his hand gently down her back. "The last I heard, Johnny was still sleeping a lot."

"He's getting better. Raylene Walker and I were there today, and he seemed much more relaxed and more alert than yesterday."

He pulled her to him and kissed her. "Can't this wait until tomorrow?"

She shook her head. "I can't relax, thinking what I've been thinking."

He pushed himself to his feet. "How about if I call the hospital and talk to Wendy, see how she feels about it." Without waiting for a reply, he went into the house to the kitchen phone. Tess followed, and after a brief conversation with the nurse, Luke hung up. "Wendy's sound asleep

in the family waiting room and Johnny is resting comfortably. Whatever you want to talk to Johnny about can wait
until tomorrow."

"You're probably right," Tess admitted, "but what if
you're wrong?"

"I have no idea what you're talking about, love."

"I know. Just let me make a phone call."

She went to her office and looked up the number she
wanted. The woman who answered sounded cross. Tess
had probably awakened her. After informing Tess that the
party she asked for wasn't available, she disconnected with
a bang.

He wasn't at home, but that didn't mean . . .

Tess dropped the receiver into the cradle and hurried out
of the office. "Luke," she called, "I'm going to the hospital.
You can wait here for me if you'd rather."

"No, I'll come with you. Afterward, we can take a drive
out to the lake."

They took Luke's car. "Are you going to tell me what's
got you so agitated?" he asked as he pulled away from Iris
House.

"I'd rather not say just yet. If I'm wrong, which I hope I
am, I'll feel silly if I've worried you for nothing."

"And you think Johnny can tell you whether you're right
or not?"

"I hope so."

"Does this have anything to do with Julian Walker's
murder?"

"I don't know."

"If so, there's a good chance, Tess, that Johnny won't be
able to tell you anything helpful."

"I have to try, Luke."

At the hospital, Tess insisted on getting off at the floor
below Johnny's and taking the stairs the rest of the way.

Luke shook his head, but followed her to the stairs. "I
know what you're up to, honey. You're afraid the nurse

won't let you disturb a patient at this hour, so you think you can slip in from the other end of the hall."

"Exactly," Tess told him as she pushed open the door to the stairs.

Johnny's floor was quiet, most of the light concentrated in the area of the nurses' station. The lights in the hallway outside the patient rooms had been dimmed.

Just as they stepped away from the stairwell door, a nurse came out from behind the nurses' station, crossed the hall, and entered a small room where employees took their coffee breaks. Tess grabbed Luke's hand and pressed back into the shadows. She hadn't come this far to have a nurse turn her away at the door.

A few minutes later, the nurse came out of the break room and returned to her chair at the nurses' station. They hesitated another moment, then Tess whispered, "Wait here." Tess crept forward far enough to see that the nurse was alone behind the desk. She was sipping her soft drink and reading a paperback book.

Tess gestured for Luke to follow her as she tiptoed down the hall to Johnny's room. The door was closed. The sign on the door had been turned with the "No Visitors" side out. The other side of the sign said "Short Visits Only, Please." That was the side that had been showing the last time Tess had visited, and she paused, but only for a moment.

She pushed gently on the door, opening it a crack, and looked in. The only light in the room was a tiny bulb in one corner, which left the bed in deep shadow. Tess heard movement. Johnny must be having a restless night.

She stood there, waiting for her eyes to adjust to the darkness. There seemed to be a bulky shadow above the bed. What . . . ? She pushed the door farther back. It was another moment before it dawned on her what she was looking at.

"Oh, dear God!" she said.

The form moved, changed shape. Tess fumbled madly beside the door for a light switch while Luke went around her into the room.

"What's happening here?" he demanded.

Tess's fingers finally found the switch, and she turned on the light. A man leaned over Johnny's bed, his back to the door. He was pressing a pillow to Johnny's face. The sound Tess had heard was Johnny struggling for air.

Luke ran forward, grabbed the man, shoved him aside, and pulled the pillow off Johnny, who took great, gasping gulps of air.

Tess was staring at Wayne Trammell, who had fallen against the foot of the bed with a grunt of pain when Luke shoved him. His face was gray, his mouth slack. And his eyes were not the friendly eyes Tess was accustomed to seeing. Instead, they looked desperate.

The nurse, having heard the commotion, came running into the room. "What are you people doing in here?"

"Saving your patient's life," Tess told her.

"What?" The nurse looked from Wayne to Luke and then at the pillow Luke had thrown on the floor. Johnny was still breathing heavily. The nurse began checking his vital signs.

"Leave the room," the nurse barked. "All of you. The patient needs his rest." Tess realized the nurse had yet to comprehend what had really happened there.

Wayne Trammell stood at the end of the bed, his legs spread, his arms hanging at his sides. "Get out of my way, Fredrik. I'm leaving." The raspy tone of his voice made the nurse turn to stare at him.

"You'll have to go through me if you do," Luke said.

"Nobody's leaving till the police get here," Tess said. "I'll go and call them."

"He—he tried to kill me," Johnny rasped.

The nurse's mouth dropped. She looked as if she might faint.

*   *   *

Thirty minutes later, Chief Butts and Officer Andy Neill had arrived, listened to Tess and Luke explain what had happened, and arrested Trammell. Neill handcuffed him and took him to the city jail. During the entire process, Trammell opened his mouth only once, to say that he wanted a lawyer.

The nurse had pronounced Johnny none the worse physically for his near-death experience. "But he's strung out emotionally," she added, "as anybody would be." After Trammell was removed, she said, "Mr. Linzy was remarkably better today. He's been awake most of the time and talking a blue streak. I hope this doesn't bring on a relapse." She frowned as she left the room, saying she'd check back shortly.

"Thank you, Tess, Luke," Johnny said, his voice hoarse. It was at least the tenth time he'd thanked them. "I talked Wendy into taking a nap in the family waiting room. The nurse was supposed to wake her if I had any visitors."

"Wayne must have come up the stairs so he wouldn't have to pass the nurses' station," Tess said.

"If you hadn't come when you did—why did you come, anyway?"

"I'd like to know that myself," Butts put in.

"Me, too," Luke added, and Butts gave him a funny look.

"It's a long story," Tess said.

"Linzy here might need to rest, but I got all night," Butts said.

"No, I want to hear," Johnny said.

"It has to do with some land the country club wants to buy for a new golf course. Oliver Stedman, who's staying at Iris House, owns it, but I learned today that the land is really held in the name of a corporation, which is owned by Oliver and a partner. My father and Oliver are old friends from college days, yet Oliver has never mentioned the corporation to my father. That made me curious so I asked some questions. Even Oliver's wife, Ruth, didn't know who the partner was."

"You think it's Wayne Trammell?" Butts asked.

Tess nodded. "I thought about it all day, and it's the only thing that made any sense."

"No wonder they were keeping quiet about Wayne's partnership," Luke said. "Wayne's chairman of the board—that's a definite conflict of interest. I must say I'm disappointed in Oliver."

"I'm sure Wayne convinced him it was kosher," Tess said. "Wayne has been pressing the board to buy Oliver's land for months, even though there's another suitable site with a lower price tag." She glanced at Johnny. "Wayne even got Johnny to campaign for the higher-priced site."

Johnny sighed heavily. "He offered me seventy-five thousand dollars if I could convince the board to buy the land. I needed the money—or I thought I did. But, after what happened the night of the barbecue . . ."

"Wayne killed Julian Walker," Tess said. It wasn't a question. "I don't know why, but I'm sure it had something to do with the land deal."

"That night, Wayne and I met in the green room to discuss it again," Johnny said. "Wayne was keeping the pressure on me to talk to the board members who were undecided about which site to buy. He kept reminding me that it was the easiest seventy-five thousand I'd ever make. We didn't know that Julian was in the pantry—until he walked in on us and said he knew what we were up to and that he wanted in on the money, too. He demanded another seventy-five thousand to keep quiet about what he knew."

"So you and Trammell decided to kill him," Butts snarled.

"*No!*" Frantically, Johnny tried to sit up, but he fell back exhausted. As soon as he caught his breath, he said, "I swear I had nothing to do with that. About an hour after Julian barged in on us, I realized Wayne had disappeared again. He'd been acting really nervous ever since Julian made his demand. When he returned to the kitchen, I went in search of him and walked into the green room right after he'd stabbed Walker. He'd heard Julian in the pantry and called him into the green room to reason with him, but Julian continued to demand money. Wayne had picked up a knife from the pantry—just to scare Julian, he said. But Julian wouldn't back down, so Wayne stabbed him. He swore he never planned it. He was beside himself. He yelled at me to grab Walker's feet before blood got on the carpet, and we carried him into the pantry. I didn't know what else to do. I was terrified Wayne would turn on me."

"And he was the one who tried to run you down with his car, right?" Tess asked.

"Yeah. After that night, when I helped him carry Walker's body to the pantry, that's all I could think about. I couldn't sleep. I could hardly eat. I wanted to go to the police but I was afraid to. Finally, I met with Wayne at the country club—it was the night that you came to see me, Tess. Wayne had just left when you walked in. I'd told him I didn't want the money, that I wanted nothing more to do with the land deal or him. I know he was afraid I would go to the police, though I never said that in so many words. So he planned to make sure I never talked. He caught me as I walked home and plowed into me with his car."

"So that didn't work," Butts said, "and he came here tonight to finish the job."

"I guess Wayne heard you'd come out of the coma," Luke said.

"He called to check on Johnny and even came to visit," Tess said. "Wendy told me. He had no way of knowing that Johnny had been conscious since the day after the hit-and-run. But the secret's been out for twenty-four hours or so."

"He must've figured," Butts mused, "that he had to kill you in your bed before you had a chance to point a finger at him."

"And he almost succeeded," Johnny said wearily. He glanced around the room. "Where's my wife?"

"Asleep in the family waiting room," Tess said.

"Good. Don't wake her. Tomorrow is soon enough for

her to learn about what happened. I'd like to tell her myself, Chief, if that's all right with you. I've got some heavy explaining to do."

"You still aren't out of the woods as far as I'm concerned," Butts told him. "You helped cover up a murder, Linzy."

Johnny swallowed hard. "I know, but I'm glad it's all out in the open. Now I just hope I can save my marriage."

Chapter 26

As it turned out, Wendy Linzy rallied behind her husband. When Tess visited Johnny again the next day, Wendy followed her into the hall to say, "I blame myself for Johnny ever considering taking Wayne Trammell up on his offer in the first place. If he hadn't been so worried about how much money I was spending, he would never have considered helping Wayne sell that land to the club."

Tess thought she was being too hard on herself. "It was his decision, Wendy."

"But he was under such stress," she protested. "Now he's worried that Chief Butts is going to charge him with helping Wayne cover up the murder."

"That could happen," Tess told her, "but with a good defense attorney, Johnny might get off with probation."

"My father's already talked to a criminal defense lawyer in Kansas City. I haven't had the nerve to tell Johnny yet. I want to wait until he's stronger, but I don't see how he can turn down my father's help under the circumstances."

Wendy might actually want to cut the financial apron strings to her father, but he was still the first person she ran to in time of trouble. Tess suspected the Linzy marriage was in for more tough times.

She said good-bye and headed back to Iris House, where Gertie was making a double recipe of her famous To-Die-For Chocolate Dessert, the one that should have won that cooking contest, if Julian Walker hadn't added salt to Gertie's sugar canister.

Tess had met Gertie at the back door that morning when she arrived for work to give her the news that Wayne Trammell had been arrested for Walker's murder. She could actually see the weight of worry roll off Gertie's shoulders.

Oliver and Ruth were informed of the arrest at breakfast, along with Tess's family.

"How in the world did he get away with it as long as he did?" Frank asked. "You'd think he'd have had blood on him somewhere."

"I'm sure his clothes were bloody," Tess said, "but you said when he bought clothes, he always bought several of the same shirt or pants exactly alike, to keep from having to shop again soon. And he kept extra clothes in his club locker—for the odd occasion when he spent the night in the locker room. He must've had duplicates of what he was wearing that night in his locker."

"I've seen several shirts and trousers in his locker. You must be right, Tess. He had duplicates." Frank nodded thoughtfully. "So that's how he did it. Boy, you think you know a man and then he does something totally out of character—or what you think his character is."

"I still can't believe Wayne killed that man," Oliver said. "I know it's true, but it just boggles my mind."

Ruth was studying her husband gravely. "Didn't you realize that keeping Wayne's interest in the land secret was unethical?"

Oliver sighed. "I guess, down deep, I did. But Wayne kept referring to our long friendship, and how he needed the money to get a divorce. I let him convince me."

"How long have you and Wayne owned the land?" Frank asked.

"More than fifteen years," Oliver said. "Wayne contacted me when the country club was under construction. He was sure that, with the way Victoria Springs was growing, the club would eventually have to expand its facilities and that there would be new houses built out there. It was reasonable to assume that, in time, the land would be very valuable. He told me he wanted to be a silent partner to keep Esther from finding out. I guess he was already planning to get out of the marriage eventually."

Ruth looked troubled. "Even I didn't know he was a part of that corporation."

Oliver gave her a sheepish look. "No, dear. Wayne insisted that nobody else could know."

Ruth folded her napkin and placed it beside her plate. "Well, I'm hurt. The very idea that you could keep a secret like that from me for fifteen years." She rose to leave the table.

Oliver followed her. "Ruth, I'm sorry."

"How do I know you aren't keeping other things from me?"

"I swear I'm not. The corporation only owned that one piece of land, which I'm sure the country club won't buy, the way things have turned out."

"It serves you right, Oliver," Ruth said. "Now you won't be able to retire as soon as we'd hoped." It was the last thing Tess heard as the couple went up the stairs to their room.

"Wayne can be very persuasive," Frank murmured. "But Oliver knows that as well as I. He should never have let Wayne suck him in."

"I'm sure Ruth will be pointing that out to him for some time to come," Zelda observed.

"I don't understand exactly what happened," Madison put in.

"Me, neither," Curt added. "Except Mr. Trammell killed the chef and Gertie's not going to get arrested."

"That's one good thing that came out of this," Frank

said. "Tess, I still don't see how you knew Wayne was going to try to kill Linzy last night."

"I hoped it wasn't true," Tess admitted. "I just couldn't rid myself of the suspicion, especially after I called Wayne's house and learned he wasn't home."

"But what made you suspect Wayne in the first place?" Frank asked.

"I'd begun to suspect that Wayne was Oliver's partner in the land ownership, and that he had somehow gotten Johnny to campaign for its purchase with the board. Then I began to wonder if Julian Walker had also been involved somehow, and if that had anything to do with his death. I knew that only two people could tell me: Wayne and Johnny. I couldn't get hold of Wayne, and that made me anxious about Johnny's safety. Thank goodness Luke and I reached him in time!"

"I'm very sorry all this had to happen right before your wedding, dear," her father said.

"I'm just glad it's over. And speaking of the wedding," Tess said, "I have a busy day ahead of me. Imagine, just five days left."

Chapter 27

On her wedding day, Tess took a mug of coffee out to her patio to watch the sun rise. A yellow glow appeared on the horizon, expanded like a huge balloon being blow up, slowly turning orange and red. For a few moments, she cleared her mind of the many tasks awaiting her attention and, eyes closed, felt calm stealing over her.

It was going to be a lovely day. Gertie was no longer a murder suspect, and she was about to marry the only man she'd ever loved.

The fabric of silence was torn when Maddie, still in her nightshirt, came around the house searching for her. "Oh, here you are, big sister. Happy wedding day."

"Thank you, sweetie." Tess patted the cushion beside her. "Come and sit with me for a minute."

Madison curled up on the cushion, drawing her legs up and stretching the knit fabric of her nightshirt over them. "You're not supposed to go to the kitchen yet. Gertie is cooking up a special breakfast. Between us, it's a fancy casserole. A French recipe, Gertie said."

"I hope I can eat," Tess said. "I'm starting to get butterflies."

"Everything is going to be great, Tess. Don't worry." She sounded so grown up that Tess had to laugh.

They sat there together until Zelda came out to tell them that breakfast was ready. From then on, things seemed to speed up, as though somebody were running a video on fast forward. Tess would never forget her first sight of the church sanctuary resplendent with the beautiful flowers Dahlia had insisted on providing.

As soon as they arrived at the church, she'd peeked into the sanctuary from the small waiting room off the foyer. The florist had arranged white wrought-iron railings entwined with green ivy around the raised area where the bride and groom would stand during the ceremony. Huge bouquets of daisies and salmon-colored roses with yellow satin streamers decorated the front of the sanctuary, and small bouquets bedecked the end of each pew along the center aisle.

"Oh," Tess gasped to Cinny and Maddie, who had accompanied her to the church, "Aunt Dahlia has really outdone herself."

"Wow, it's beautiful," Maddie agreed.

"Hey, I helped Mother arrange the flowers," Cinny said. "She got me up at the crack of dawn and dragged me down here to meet the florist. I barely got home in time to change and pick up you two."

Tess opened her arms to hug her cousin. "Thank you, Cinny." She reached out to pull Maddie into the embrace. "You, too, Maddie."

"For what?"

"Just for being my sister and my maid of honor." Tess released them and smoothed the front of her gown. "Anybody got a tissue?" she sniffed.

Cinny grabbed one from her purse. "Don't you dare cry and mess up your mascara."

Tess chuckled and patted her eyes. "I keep forgetting that I'm wearing it."

"Yeah." Maddie grinned. "I helped her put it on. Can you believe she never wears mascara?"

"I can," Cinny told her, "and, Maddie, I hope you'll come back and help me get ready for my wedding."

Maddie's eyes bulged. "*Your* wedding?"

Cinny's hand flew to her mouth. "Oops."

Maddie shrieked. "You and Cody are getting married!"

"Shh," Tess cautioned. "It's a secret. They haven't even set the date yet."

"I didn't want to tell Mother till after Tess and Luke's wedding," Cinny said. "Swear you won't breathe a word to a soul, Maddie."

"But when are you going to tell Aunt Dahlia and Uncle Maurice?"

"Maybe tomorrow. Can you keep quiet until then?"

Maddie huffed, offended. "Of course I can." A smile tugged at her lips. "Provided you let me be there when you tell them. I *have* to see Aunt Dahlia's reaction."

Cinny looked at Tess. "Your sister is a master manipulator, for one of such tender years."

"I know," Tess agreed, "but she's the only sister I have, so I think I'll keep her."

They heard voices in the foyer. Guests were beginning to arrive. Cinny hurriedly closed the waiting room door. "Can't let anyone see the bride before the ceremony."

Tess glanced at the clock on the wall. "Only ten minutes now." She blinked back tears."

"Oh, Lord, she's at it again," Maddie said.

"I'm just so happy," Tess said. And then they heard the first strains of the organ.

Soon Cinny picked up her nosegay of daisies and satin streamers and slipped out of the room, followed shortly by Maddie. And then Tess's father peeked in. "Ah, Tess, you're a vision. You look so like your mother, standing there."

She moved to the door and kissed his cheek. "Thank you, Dad."

And then, with her bridal bouquet in one hand and her

other hand linked through her father's arm, she was walking down the aisle. Then her gaze met Luke's and she saw nothing but his handsome face, his blue eyes shining with love.

The wedding went off without a hitch, and Paula Overton handled the reception with enthusiasm and great efficiency, as though she'd been catering weddings for years.

Several of the guests tried to pump Tess and Luke about the night they caught Wayne Trammell trying to kill Johnny Linzy. They turned these attempts aside, saying they didn't want to dwell on unhappy thoughts on their wedding day.

By the time Tess had changed into her going-away suit, a lovely champagne-colored silk chambray, weariness, happiness, and excitement had merged into elation so high she felt her feet were touching the ground only about half the time.

Then she and Luke were running to his car through a rain of rice. Luke's groomsmen had tied tin cans on the back bumper and painted "Just Married" on the back window, so their trip out of town was clamorous enough to bring people out on the sidewalk to wave and shout good wishes. As soon as they cleared the city limits, Luke got rid of the cans.

Snuggled next to him on the drive to the Springfield airport, Tess let the tension drain out of her and enjoyed the glow of happiness that seemed to have enveloped them.

Luke reached for her hand. "I love you, wife."

"And I adore you, husband," she murmured.

"Tired?"

She smiled. "A little, but I can rest on the plane. Can't you tell me now where we're going?"

"As soon as we're airborne."

"You love teasing me, don't you?"

"I just want to prolong the suspense."

"Maybe I already know where we're going."

"Oh, yeah? Where?"

"A cruise."

He glanced at her in surprise. "How'd you—"

"I remember telling you several months ago that I'd like to take an Alaskan cruise."

He laughed. "Well, you got it half-right."

"Which half?"

"The cruise part."

"Well, I assumed we weren't going to Alaska when you told me to bring my passport. So where *are* we going?"

"I'll tell you when we're on the plane."

She tried but could not get him to reveal anything else until they were belted into their seats and the plane left the runway. Then he pulled a brochure from his carry-on bag and handed it to her. "We're flying to London first and will spend a couple of nights there. Then we hook up with the cruise group."

"A Scandinavian cruise? Oh, Luke! This is marvelous."

"They have a honeymoon cabin on the top deck. They guarantee we'll be treated royally."

"We even have stops in Germany and St. Petersburg. Then, we go to"—she glanced down the itinerary—"Helsinki, Stockholm, Copenhagen, Oslo, and back to London. Twelve days! Oh, Luke, this is going to be heavenly."

He took her hand and brought it to his lips. Sighing, she rested her head on the headrest and pushed her chair back to a comfortable position. Luke had booked them first-class, so there was ample room without crowding the person seated behind her.

After a moment, Luke whispered in her ear, "You asleep, Mrs. Fredrik?"

She didn't open her eyes. "Uh-huh. I'm having a lovely dream in which my husband plays a starring role."

He pushed his seat back until it was parallel with hers. Sighing, he murmured, "I think I'll join you in that dream."

Iris House Recipes

SMOKED BRISKET
Serves 12–15

Hickory chips
½ cup sugar
¼ cup paprika
2 tablespoons salt
2 tablespoons pepper
1 tablespoon garlic powder
1 (4- to 5-pound) beef brisket

Soak hickory chips in water overnight. Prepare charcoal fire by piling charcoal in one end of grill; let burn 15 to 20 minutes or until flames disappear and coals are white. Add 6 to 8 pieces of soaked hickory to coals.

Mix well sugar, paprika, salt, pepper, and garlic powder in a bowl. Rub brisket with dry mixture. Place brisket on rack away from coals on opposite end of grill; cover with grill hood. Partially open air vents (about halfway).

Cook brisket 1 hour; wrap in heavy-duty aluminum foil. Return brisket to grill; cover and cook an additional 30 minutes or to desired degree of doneness. Place additional hickory chips on coals, if necessary.

STUFFED CHICKEN BREASTS
Serves 2

*2 large skinless, boneless chicken breast halves
    (about ²/₃ pound)*
¼ cup chopped onion
3 tablespoons chopped green pepper
1 small clove garlic, minced
2 tablespoons butter or margarine, melted
²/₃ cup herb-seasoned stuffing mix
⅓ cup water
¼ teaspoon salt
2 tablespoons butter or margarine, melted
½ cup cream of chicken soup, undiluted
2 tablespoons dry white wine
1 tablespoon herb-seasoned stuffing mix
Chopped fresh parsley

Place each piece of chicken between 2 sheets of waxed paper; flatten to ¼-inch thickness, using a rolling pin. Set aside.

Saute onion, green pepper, and minced garlic in 2 tablespoons butter. Stir in ²/₃ cup stuffing mix, water, salt, and pepper.

Spread stuffing mixture evenly on each chicken breast, leaving a ½-inch margin on all sides. Fold short ends of chicken over stuffing; roll up and secure with wooden toothpicks.

Brown chicken in 2 tablespoons butter. Place in a 9-inch pie pan.

Combine soup and wine; pour over chicken. Sprinkle with 1 tablespoon stuffing mix. Cover with aluminum foil, and bake at 325 degrees for 50 minutes or until done. Garnish with chopped parsley.

VEGETABLE MEDLEY
Serves 4

1½ cups broccoli flowerets
1½ cups sliced zucchini
½ cup red pepper strips
½ cup sliced water chestnuts
¼ cup sliced green onions
2 teaspoons chicken-flavored bouillon granules
2 tablespoons butter or margarine

Combine broccoli, zucchini, red pepper, water chestnuts, and green onions in a shallow 2-quart casserole; sprinkle with bouillon granules and toss. Dot with butter. Cover tightly with heavy-duty plastic wrap; fold back a small corner of wrap to allow steam to escape. Microwave on high 2 minutes; give dish a half-turn and microwave on high additional 2 minutes. Let stand, covered, 5 minutes.

GERTIE'S TO-DIE-FOR CHOCOLATE DESSERT
Serves 10–12

16 (1-ounce) squares semisweet chocolate
⅔ cup butter or margarine
5 eggs, beaten
2 tablespoons sugar
2 tablespoons all-purpose flour
Raspberry Sauce
Whipped cream
Fresh raspberries

Generously grease and flour sides and bottom of a 9-inch springform pan.

Place chocolate and butter in top of a double boiler; bring water to a boil. Reduce heat to low; cook until chocolate and butter melt. Gradually add chocolate mixture to eggs, beating at medium speed of an electric mixer 10 minutes. Fold in sugar and flour. Pour into prepared pan. Bake at 400 degrees for 15 minutes. (Cake will not be set in center.) Chill. Spoon about 3 tablespoons Raspberry Sauce on each dessert plate; place wedge of chocolate dessert on sauce. Garnish with whipped cream and fresh raspberries.

RASPBERRY SAUCE

2 cups fresh raspberries
2 cups water
¼ cup sugar
2 tablespoons cornstarch
2 tablespoons water

Combine raspberries, 2 cups water, and ¼ cup sugar in a large saucepan, and bring to a boil. Reduce heat, and let mixture simmer 30 minutes. Put raspberry mixture through a sieve, discard seeds. Return raspberry mixture to saucepan, and set aside.

Combine cornstarch and 2 tablespoons water in a bowl, stirring until mixture is smooth. Add cornstarch mixture to raspberry mixture. Cook over medium heat, stirring constantly, until mixture comes to a boil. Cook 1 additional minute, stirring constantly. Remove mixture from heat, and let cool thoroughly.

Tasty mysteries by
Joanne Pence
Featuring culinary queen Angie Amalfi

TO CATCH A COOK
0-06-103085-6/$5.99 US/$7.99 Can
Angie gets mixed up in a deadly stew of family secrets, missing gems, and murder in another tasty mystery that blends fine dining and detection.

And Don't Miss

A COOK IN TIME
0-06-104454-7/$5.99 US/$7.99 Can

COOKS OVERBOARD
0-06-104453-9/$5.99 US/$7.99 Can

COOK'S NIGHT OUT
0-06-104396-6/$5.99 US/$7.99 Can

COOKING MOST DEADLY
0-06-104395-8/$5.99 US/$7.99 Can

COOKING UP TROUBLE
0-06-108200-7/$5.99 US/$7.99 Can

SOMETHING'S COOKING
0-06-108096-9/$5.99 US/$7.99 Can

TOO MANY COOKS
0-06-108199-X/$5.99 US/$7.99 Can

....

Murder Is on the Menu
at the Hillside Manor Inn
Bed-and-Breakfast Mysteries by
MARY DAHEIM
featuring Judith McMonigle Flynn